consequences...

Laurie Depp

consequences...

Don't call me baby

Hodder
Children's
Books

A division of Hachette Children's Book

Hodder Children's Books
a division of Hachette Children's Books
338 Euston Road, London NW1 3BH
An Hachette Livre UK Company

1

You've heard people talk about the 'pivotal moment' – the exact time something really important, happens in your life. The moment that changes your life, for better or worse.

That's just happened to me.

I think.

I've got a new job.

As a nanny.

Yeah, OK, big deal. But this isn't just any old nannying job. It's *who* I'm going to be working for that makes it the you're-never-going-to-believe this, all-out-life-changing job of a lifetime.

These nanny agencies, they don't give anything away. I must have been for about eight interviews with them – four interviews for this job alone. I've filled in forms, told them my life story (well, leaving out the finer details of my not quite fabulous love life, and my little brother's hygiene issues), been police-checked(!), and grilled by Interpol – at least that's what it felt like.

I didn't mind – except that up until now I hadn't got a

clue who the clients were. Not a Scooby Doo. The agency kept going on about discretion and saying how I would have to sign a confidentiality agreement. Real cloak and dagger stuff.

I was expecting a minor royal's second cousin once removed, or maybe a foreign diplomat's daughter. Or a total D-list wannabe flexing a bit of celebrity muscle.

What I did *not* expect was the hottest, numero uno, most media-frenzy couple ever . . .

the Daily News (April 2000)

BB's New Bird

Ice-man Ballentine seems to be thawing if this pic with new chick Kassie Campbell is anything to go by. Curvy Kassie (21) works as a pole dancer at Kensington's Kitten Club – top London celebrity hangout. 'It's definitely love,' says an insider. 'Kassie's all over him and he doesn't seem to be complaining!'

C U R R I C U L U M   V I T A E

Katie Meredith
13 Sandringham Road
Hastings
East Sussex
TN34

01424 421 . . . (eve)
07949138 . . . (day)

DATE OF BIRTH: 24 August 1989
NATIONALITY: British

EDUCATIONAL QUALIFICATIONS

2005-2007 Knightsbridge Super Nannies Diploma in Childcare and Education including First Aid and Food Hygiene

The course also covered: language learning in the preschool child, Child Protections, SENCO/Inclusion training stages 1 and 2, Autistic Spectrum Disorder (ASD)

2000-2005 Helensdale School, Hastings, East Sussex

GCSEs: English Language (A), English Literature (A), German (C), History (B), Media Studies (A), Science (double award BB), Mathematics (C), Food Sciences (B), Textiles (C)

EMPLOYMENT HISTORY

SUMMER 2005/06 holiday au pair for Fiorentini family based in Naples

Two six-week placements caring for four children: two boys aged nine and six and two girls aged four and two. (The children had all aged a year by my second placement with the family.) Spending six weeks in shared charge of all children (split with their mother) including three weeks at the family home in Naples and three weeks at the holiday home in Calabria.

During my time of charge I was responsible for all aspects of the children's daily lives

4

including: morning routine of breakfasting, washing and dressing, activities throughout the day including trips out and organized play within the home. All mealtimes - for which I prepared meals from scratch using organic ingredients. Bath and bedtime routines including storytime and settling for the younger children.

WINTER 2005/06

On-site nanny

Sankt Moritz

Ski Moritz - Exclusive Hotel and Chalet Complex

Participating fully in all the nannying services the resort had to offer including: day nursery for babies and toddlers, evening babysitting service, and evening children's clubs. Supervising outdoor and indoor adventure play areas.

ADDITIONAL COURSES:

Organic cooking for children

Baby Massage

Transforming a Difficult Child

OTHER SKILLS: PC literate. Full clean driving licence.

INTERESTS: Reading and cinema-going. Keeping fit with badminton, swimming and cycling.

Mr and Mrs Fiorentini   Ski Moritz
Naples   Sankt Moritz
Italy   Switzerland

PRESENT SALARY :

Details on request

That's me. Katie Meredith. Seventeen years old (very soon to make it to the magic eighteen – at last! Faking it on the ID front is a complete pain). Qualified nanny. From a fairly standard seaside town. Daughter of Carol (teaching assistant) and Ray (plasterer), big sister to Jo (fifteen-year-old moody Goth teenage-angst-ridden freak) and Oli (twelve-year-old football-obsessive pest).

So that's my life. Or rather, that *was* my life. It's hardly going to be like that any more, is it? How can it be now that I'm the new full-time live-in nanny to Brett and Kassie Ballentine! Who, for those of you who don't know – surely there can't be anyone – are the most famous couple *ever*.

He's the highest player for London Spartacus FC and she's his ex-pole-dancer wife who is absolutely never out of the popular press. Not for anything astounding, but you know what it's like: 'Kassie Ballentine buys new Balenciaga bag', 'Kassie Ballentine changes celebrity hair stylist', 'Kassie Ballentine seen drinking a cup of coffee'. She is literally *never* out of the gossip columns and now little old me will be rubbing shoulders with her every day. And to think I probably, in some perverse way, owe my change in fortune to Josh Markham. The universe certainly moves in mysterious ways.

I suppose I'd better put you in the picture. Josh Markham was my first love. And I don't mean holding hands in primary school or even snogging behind the bike sheds-type thing. This was no schoolgirl infatuation. This was love with a capital L. Everyone was saying 'you're too young' and 'you don't want to get too serious too soon'. But it's not like I could help it, not when I looked into his eyes and felt like my heart was about to burst out of my chest. If someone merely mentioned Josh's name my pulse rate would go up. I was absolutely smitten. And he was smitten with me. For one whole blissful year. And then he cheated on me with Megan Lowry and the bottom fell out of my world.

I mean serious devastation. We'd finished school. The whole summer holidays were stretching ahead of us. I was imagining lazy summer days lying on the beach together, strolling along the prom, laughing as our ice creams dripped down to our elbows and suddenly . . . It was over. I was his ex. His stupid, no-one-could-possibly-fancy-me hideous ex.

Everyone was really supportive.

'Plenty more fish in the sea,' said my mum.

Who wants a fish? I want him.

'He was so up himself anyway, you deserve someone so much better,' said Carly (best mate extraordinaire).

Yeah, maybe I liked up-himself and I don't want anyone else, I want Josh.

'You come round and see me and Grandad we'll have a nice game of Scrabble and cheer you up,' Nan told me.

Yeah, and remind me of the fact that you've been together for ever and I couldn't even make it past a year with the man of my dreams.

'Have ten quid, buy yourself something nice,' suggested Dad.

Aaaaarrrrgh!

I digress. The point is, Josh kind of forced a life re-assessment on me. A change in direction. When I was with him I was quite happy to stay in Hastings. Go to the local college, get a job there. He was doing a modern apprenticeship – training to be an electrician – and I've always really loved children so childcare seemed like the obvious option for me. All our mates are here, the nightlife in Hastings ain't great but it ain't that bad either and I guess, ultimately, I had a sad little fantasy about us settling down into some sort of domestic bliss, proving everyone wrong and ending up like Nan and Grandad nestled snuggly together in a little bungalow, kids scattered not too far away and roses growing neatly round the door.

And then he ruined it. Initially I spent all my time crying, and refusing to come out of my room. But once I'd realized the ultimate futility of that line of action I had some big decisions to make. Every time I went out I was on tenterhooks – desperate to see Josh and yet, at the same time, desperate not to. Seeing Megan Lowry draped over him like a cheap wrap didn't exactly light my fire. So it got to the point where I saw that if I wasn't going to get over him (not likely in the foreseeable future) I either had to become a hermit or I had to make a fresh start. I chose option number two. So, weirdly enough, thanks, Josh – you did me one helluva favour.

I didn't go to the local college. Oh no. I found *the* most prestigious childcare college in the country and went for that. I did my research. Found out what they were looking for in a candidate and got myself the place.

My block-out-Josh strategy was to do stuff that was bigger, better and more exciting, leaving no room for him in my head, or in my heart. Well, I certainly achieved that. I took every opportunity to get more experience – which sometimes was really scary and hard – but it was me saying, 'Sod you, Josh – look at me now!'

Of course there were lots of tears along the way – even applying for this job was scary. Having to put myself forward and act all confident and self-assured. But, I guess, putting on a brave face and really going for it has finally paid off, big style.

You see, I'm not what you'd call academic. School was never really my thing, but I'm not stupid either and I know I'm good with kids. I've always felt really comfortable around them.

And now? Now I'm responsible, to some degree, for how two little human beings are going to turn out. Two little Ballentines. Me? Scared? I'm bricking it.

Hello!

Exclusive at the Celebrity Wedding of the Year (June 2000)

Model Kassie Campbell (21) met gorgeous London Spartacus FC star Brett Ballentine at the popular Kitten Club where she worked as a dancer. 'It was love at first sight,' purrs Kassie, and from the way Brett looks at her I'd say it still is. To say they've had a whirlwind romance would be an understatement but as Brett succinctly put it at the reception: 'When you feel this sure about something . . . why wait!'

Kassie arrived at Linton Castle in Sussex in a pink Rolls Royce. She wore a beautiful, diamond-encrusted, ivory silk dress with a 30-foot train. Celebrity guests included a number of Brett's footballing colleagues (with glamorous WAGs in tow) and a whole host of other A-listers as well as over five hundred close personal friends.

The couple presided over their reception on matching pink thrones and overwhelmed their guests after the speeches with the surprise announcement that Kassie is three months pregnant with their first child. Perhaps it's a good job he rushed her up the aisle. After all, soon that frock simply wouldn't fit!

3

Telling my family the news went pretty much as expected. Mum was shocked, then thrilled, then manic. And Jo, who makes it her life's mission to appear completely unmoved by anything, got slightly animated at the news. And Oli, I thought he was actually going to wet himself he got that excited. He started reeling off figures about how many caps Brett's got – I so know nothing about football, for a sec I thought he was referring to the baseball variety! – and rumoured transfers, and player fees . . . and that's when I did start paying a bit of attention.

Oli reckons Brett could earn up to £300,000 per week. Yes, you did hear me right – *per week*. £300,000 for chasing a ball around a big field. I'm actually quietly freaked out by that, but hey, I guess I'm going to have to learn to live with it – quite literally.

And then there was Carly. I thought I was going to burst waiting for her to come round. I mean, there are some people I felt weird about telling – the Ballentines being as famous as they are and everything – but Carly knows what I'm like. She's been my best friend for for ever and, I know, whatever happens she'll always have my back. Even with the Josh thing. I know she can be harsh about him, but I also know she does it because she was so angry and upset about how hurt I was. She hated him for doing that to me. And that's gotta count for something. Plus she put up with me being a bit AWOL when Josh and I were together. We were so loved up, I hardly saw Carly but she never threw it back in my face. And, if I do get too cocky, I know she'll pull me straight back down to earth. But even she might flip with this bit of hot goss.

But first, I had to swear her to secrecy.

We were up in my room, hot chocolate in hand and marshmallows for dunking. My mum had been all coy when Carly got here. 'Come to hear the big news then?' she said to Carly, smiling at me conspiratorially.

I laughed. I mean, it's not like I'm forbidden from telling anyone and I can hardly keep it a secret for ever, but the agency don't want the information leaking to any of the press. Seems a bit far-fetched to me, but they said it was more for my sake really – I think they're worried I'll freak out if I leave the house and there are like five members of the pappy press trying to get shots of me. Bizarre as that idea seems now, I don't want to mess things up before I even start the job, so it's probably best to keep a lid on everything until I'm actually there – but I tell you, it's going to be a long month.

Carly perched on the edge of my bed. She works for a hairdresser's in downtown Hastings. This week her hair was a kind of black-and-white two-tone affair. It had a couple of layers in it, the peroxide blonde hair underneath with the almost jet black on top – like an uber-fashionable skunk. Carly changes her hair colour on a weekly basis – she likes to keep ahead of the 'trends'. Today she was wearing skinny jeans and a Ramones T-shirt with a pair of baseball boots – again, looking cool without trying too hard. Effortlessly cool, I guess is what you'd call it.

Anyway, Carly and secrecy – what can I say, not exactly her strong point. I had to really impress on her quite how important this actually was.

'Look, Carls, when I tell you this, you've got to swear to be discreet. This is strictly confidential.' I tapped the side of my nose melodramatically.

Carly looked at me aghast. 'What do you take me for, Katie? I can be discreet! Just how famous are these people, anyway? It's not TomKat, is it?'

I shook my head in a wouldn't-you-like-to-know kind of way.

Carly grinned. 'Ooooh, interesting. Let me see. Rock god 'n' goddess with little baby rocklets.'

'Maybe.' I smiled and paused for effect.

Carly grabbed me by the shoulders. 'Come on, Katie Meredith, spill or your teddy gets it.'

What the hell, I couldn't keep it in any longer anyway . . . 'So, if I were to say to you Brett and Kassie Ballent—'

'NO!' Carly's scream drowned out the rest of my sentence. I guess the news was pretty impressive after all.

Half an hour later and I was still filling Carly in on all the details – which wasn't easy as she kept mock swooning back on the bed and screeching like a banshee.

'So then you met them – ohmygod! – in the flesh!'

I'd been telling her about the final interview. The clincher. I think they were putting me to the ultimate test as they still hadn't told me who the elusive clients were. I had to walk into the room at this posh hotel and there they were: Kassie and Brett Ballentine.

'I think,' I told Carly, 'they wanted to see if I'd pass out or scream or throw myself down at their feet or something. But I was totally cool – as a cucumber.'

Carly looked at me in disbelief.

'Yeah, I know,' I confessed. 'Amazing, right? But Carly, inside I was bricking it. And then I shook hands with Brett Ballentine – BRETT BALLENTINE!' Carly fell back on to the bed (again) laughing. 'I thought I was going to have a heart attack. Inside my head I was going, "Calm down, no big deal, pretend they're just Mr and Mrs Bloggs. It's just like any other interview." It was mad!'

It had been bizarre really. There was ordinary Katie Meredith from Hastings in this swanky London hotel with two of the most famous people in the western world. The room was amazing. High ceilings, swathes of fabric everywhere you looked, huge vases of freshly cut flowers, beautiful bone-china tea service, carved wood and gold leaf – it was like a sensual overload. I kept having to remind myself I'd done glamorous before. When I spent my summer with the Fiorentinis it was all swish hotels and staff shuffling around trying to be there without actually *being* there, if you see what I mean. And, you know what, I got quite a taste for it. That's the funny thing about being the nanny. Whereas other staff are in the real 'upstairs/downstairs' thing, the nanny's on a slightly different level. Especially these days when people are meant to be seen to actually enjoy hanging out with their kids.

The Fiorentinis were lovely. The parents were so friendly and supportive, it was like being paid to be part of their family. But it's always wise to remember that if push comes to shove, you're not a family member who'll be forgiven and the misdemeanour just shrugged off if you put a foot wrong. At the end of the day, you're still the paid help and you can always be replaced. But it never felt that stark with the Fiorentinis and I just hoped the Ballentines would be the same.

'This is so unreal,' Carly interrupted my thoughts. 'Everyone in the world knows who they are . . . and you're going to be right in the middle of their lives.' She was serious for a moment. 'Be careful, Katie, won't you?'

I looked at her, confused. 'What do you mean?'

'Well, it's just . . . you know . . . They're not exactly like the rest of us, are they? I suppose I'm just trying to say, don't go changing.' She grimaced as if she had a bad taste in her mouth. 'God, I can't believe I just said that!' She paused. 'Must be weird being famous. I mean, they must have people sucking up to them all the time just because of who they are. And let's face it, Kassie Ballentine, she's nothing in her own right, is she?'

'God, I hope my room's not bugged,' I laughed. 'I'm meant to be being discreet, not slagging off the boss before I even get there.' Carly went to speak again but I stopped her. 'I know what you mean, Carly, and you're right. Fran from the agency is usually this emotionless android. But when she introduced them she was all giggly and simpering . . . I won't be like that.' Carly raised her eyebrows at me. 'I won't!' I protested. 'You won't let me!'

Carly picked up my pillow and threw it at me. 'Too right I won't. So, go get me more hot chocolate. NOW!'

Close-Up magazine

Ballentines in Baby Heartbreak

Kassie and Brett Ballentine have been heartbroken to have to announce the loss of their first baby only two weeks after announcing Kassie's pregnancy at their £2 million wedding. It's believed Kassie miscarried shortly after arriving home from their honeymoon in the exclusive Caribbean island of Mustique.

3

So, this is it, first day of new job.

First day of new life.

It's been tough the last few days, not being able to shout it from the rooftops. Mum's been telling everyone at work that I've got a job with some posh couple in London. Which is sort of true (although I'm not sure 'posh' is actually the right word to use in connection with Kassie) and just skirting over the other bits. Like the fact that he's the most highly paid striker in the country, Spartacus football club's most sought-after player and just about the sexiest man on the planet and she's the most famous ex-pole dancer in the history of the world.

But now that I'm on my way I guess Mum'll be able to brag to her heart's content, bless her.

My dad gave me a lift to London. He insisted.

He's a man of few words is Dad, but I got the impression it was important for him to be there to send his daughter off into the big bad world of celebrity.

It's awful, I love my dad to bits but I was kind of

embarrassed. I mean, his van isn't exactly Trotters Independent Traders, but it's not a Porsche either. It's an ancient white Fiesta chugging out diesel fumes and I'm pretty sure it's only the rust that's holding it together. And Dad isn't exactly a fashion plate – his idea of dressing smartly is to put on a jumper that's a bit less stained and holey than the one he had on before. Even when he's made an effort he still looks a bit craggy and unkempt. There are times when I really think he could do with a bit of a Trinny and Susannah moment in his life.

Luckily I managed to persuade him that it would be best if he just left me and my luggage on the doorstep and went on his merry way. He didn't look too sure but I insisted. 'Dad, they're hardly going to think I'm mature and responsible enough to look after their two kids if I can't even make it to my first day of work without my dad holding my hand.'

'All right, love,' he sighed. 'If you're sure. Come here then.' He put his arms around me and gave me a big old Dad-style bear hug that always made me feel like a little girl who'd just skinned her knees.

'Bye, Dad,' I whispered. I could feel myself beginning to waver. I took a deep breath and released myself from his hold. 'See you soon,' I said, grabbing my bags and starting to clamber out of the van.

'Bye, love.' Dad waved his hand at me. 'Don't forget to give your mum a ring.'

'I won't,' I said, and watched his van disappear on to the wide London street.

I stood on the doorstep for about five minutes and tried to get my head together. I was wearing my interview suit, the smartest thing in my wardrobe: wide-legged trousers, crisp white shirt, nicely tailored jacket nipped in at the waist with a big flat stone pendant to show a bit of personality! Carly had done my hair – straight, blonde, bobbed – and it was looking about as sleek and shiny as it ever could, plus I'd spent ages applying my make-up. I mean, Kassie's face is never out of the papers. It's not that I'm in competition with her or anything, but I feel like I should at least make some sort of effort not to let the side down. But I needn't have worried too much. It wasn't like Brett or Kassie opened the door themselves. What did I expect? That Kassie would come shuffling to the door in her slippers with her Marigolds on, like I'd just caught her in the middle of doing the washing up? Wake up, Katie! I'm not even sure Kassie Ballentine even has to wipe her own bum.

Mrs Ellis, the housekeeper, opened the door. I gave her my most winning smile. I was nervous but excited too and I thought maybe she and I would be comrades – Team Ellis/Meredith helping the Ballentine household run without a hitch.

I put my hand out to shake hers – Day One of nanny school. She ignored it. Well, actually she clocked it and pulled a face like it was something fairly disgusting and turned her back to me, talking over her shoulder.

'You must be Miss Meredith,' she said, more than a touch disdainfully, and with a mere wisp of a smile. 'Please wipe your feet. Or even better, take your shoes off.' She paused to adjust something on one of the entrance-hall tables. I sort of staggered over the threshold with my bags and bent over to take my shoes off. I could feel all the blood rushing to my face.

She turned around as I was fumbling to pick up my bags and hold my shoes at the same time. 'Leave them here,' she said in a voice loaded with frustration, like she was having to deal with the biggest idiot on the planet. She must be at least sixty, at a guess. And she looks pretty good for her age, dressing in a sort of trendy older-woman way, with her hair kind of choppy and layered around her face. Not what you'd expect a housekeeper to look like – all matronly uniform with a bun in her hair – though I guess 'servants' don't look like they've come from the set of *Upstairs, Downstairs* any more. But her attitude is definitely old school. Cold and unapproachable – what's the word? Austere. Talk about having a pole up your bum. I felt like running out and getting straight on the phone to Dad. But I took a deep breath, forced a smile on my face and stood my ground.

The house is incredible. I struggled to take it all in. So many rooms – all immaculate. And Brett and Kassie's 'floor' was just amazing. Real movie-star stuff.

'You won't really spend much time here,' Mrs Ellis snapped at me (obviously thinking I had some over-blown idea about hanging out with Brett and Kassie in their bedroom!). 'But sometimes the children might come to say goodnight to their parents here so you need to get your bearings.'

She showed me their huge bedroom with a massive en suite and a walk-in wardrobe the size of our living room, all mirrored with open cupboards from floor to ceiling and pull-out racks and everything. And all the stuff was colour co-ordinated and there were about three hundred pairs of shoes in the cupboard. I would have killed to linger and have a really good gawp, but Mrs Ellis's eyes were burning into me with irritation the whole time. Like having to show me around was some kind of massive inconvenience to her. At one point she actually looked at her watch, tutted and then said, 'Well, come along,' as if I was really holding her up.

She marched me from room to room, barking out instructions. 'The children may not come in here unaccompanied and may only come in when they have been invited to do so. And I expect you to keep to the areas allocated for the use of the nanny and children.'

It was excruciating. I think I'd been kidding myself that I didn't feel that nervous, but trying to talk to her I began to realize that actually I was absolutely terrified.

I tried to win her over with a bit of small talk. I read somewhere once that people like talking about themselves. 'Have you worked for the Ballentines for long?' I asked her.

She turned her steely gaze on me, like a cobra eyeing up its prey. 'I really don't think that that's any business of yours, Miss Meredith, do you?'

Ouch! Only ten minutes in and I was beginning to wonder if I'd made a huge mistake. I had met Regan and

Maximus after I'd met Brett and Kassie (or should that be Mr and Mrs Ballentine?): the final part of the endless interview process had been a session to see how I interacted with the children, and they were lovely. But looking after them, in their own home, under the watchful eye of their parents – not to mention scary Mrs E – well, that was another matter.

She eventually showed me to my 'quarters': her word, not mine. My stuff had already been brought up by some other member of staff (I was beginning to realize that in Mrs E's eyes that's very much what I was).

'If you need anything, do come and ask,' she said. A strange grimace crossed her face – I realized it was her attempt at a smile. 'Make yourself at home and I'll see you in the playroom in half an hour.'

'Yes, Mrs Ellis.' I fought the urge to say Ma'am and curtsey. Please don't let all the staff be like her – it's like being in some Gothic horror novel.

The end of day one and I'm absolutely shattered. The kids have been lovely, but having Mrs Ellis show me the ropes was kind of nerve-wracking. I felt like she was assessing (and disapproving of) my every move.

She stood in the corner watching me, smirking a couple of times when the kids were a bit cheeky with me – cow. It made me really uncomfortable. And it was so unfair. The children were just a bit overexcited by me being there but Mrs Ellis made it seem like they were being completely over the top and that I couldn't cope. At one point Regan sort of pushed Maxi out of the way in a rush to get to me, and Maxi then fell over and instantly started squawking. Mrs Ellis was straight on it. As I tried to soothe Maxi and stop Regan's shouted explanations, she stood there all schoolmarmish and said: 'You seem very young for a position of such responsibility, Katie. I do hope you're up to the job.' Then she said, 'You may bring the children to the kitchen for dinner at five-thirty sharp,' turned on her heel and left the room.

I only hope that once I start work properly I won't have to have so much to do with her. I don't think I'll be able to hack it if I've got that old dragon breathing down my neck the whole time!

It's always weird when you first start working in someone else's house. It seems kind of rude to be riffling through their kitchen cupboards but then again, part of my job is to sort the kids' meals out . . . Although Mrs Ellis has said that if I talk to the cook we'll probably be able to come to some arrangement.

Weirder still is that I haven't actually seen Brett or Kassie yet. So it's like I haven't even had them there to say: 'Feel free to rummage through the cupboards' or 'Make yourself at home'. I'm sort of disappointed and, I guess if I'm honest with myself, a bit hurt. I thought they'd make the effort to be there on my first day and make me feel welcome. But there you go, first lesson learnt – how stupid to imagine I'm a priority to them. I'm there to make their lives easier after all. The football season's just started, of course, which is apparently why they timed my job to start now. According to the agency, when Brett wasn't playing that much over the summer he took care of the kids. He's drop-dead gorgeous is Brett, but in that mean, moody-broody kind of way. He's always been called things like 'enigmatic' or 'Ice-man Ballentine'. (Have I been obsessively reading all the gossip mags recently? Well, what do you think?) He's got a reputation as a bit of a cold fish so I can't really picture him looking after them. Still, I guess he can always kick a ball around the garden with the kids if all else fails.

Right, just time for a quick email to Carly (I know she'll just be dying to hear all the details) and then I'm hitting the sack. According to Mrs Ellis, Kassie will be here tomorrow – so I'd better get some shut-eye and try to make a good impression on my new boss.

To: carlymurphy@spscarechild.com
From: kmeredith@eggspok.com
Subject: I'm here!

Hey Carls
I'm at the Ballentines'! Kids are lovely. No sign of parents. Did swap-over with night nanny (yes you did hear me correctly), Livvy. Absolutely exhausted. Trying to take everything in and get used to my new surroundings. My flat (floor? Whatever!) is

amazing. Really plush and all mod cons – including this laptop, thank you very much. Whole house is incredible – and haven't quite got to grips with who does what amongst staff yet. So far I've come across housekeeper, Mrs Ellis (absolute evil witch from hell – but hey, that's just my first opinion!), cleaners and gardener. But Mrs E informs me there's also a PA, personal trainer, chauffeur and several other as-and-when beauty therapists, stylists, masseuses and general hangers-on, as well as a manager each for the Ballentines. Guess with all that money you've got to find something to spend it on, eh?

How's life in the salon?

I'm just going to watch a bit of telly (provided with DVD player and satellite channels!) then bath (luxury suite) and bed (gorgeous white linen). Hope I'm still here when I wake up tomorrow as really feels like complete dream!

More soon.

Lots of love

Katie xxx

Two more join Kassie's Club

We reckon Kassie Ballentine must have shares in trendy London boutique, Club. Not only is she barely seen without a Club bag over her shoulder, but she's busy converting other Spartacus wives to the cause. The Chelsea Queen of Bling was spotted last week shopping with Viv Westerley (24) and Sukie Pilkington (25), both married to husband Brett's teammates. It just goes to show Spartacus is not the only Club these girls are attached to!

4

Well, I'm really starting to get into the swing of things now. It's still summer holidays at the moment, so I've got both kids with me all the time. It'll be weird when Regan goes to school in a couple of weeks' time – I think Maxi will really miss her. Don't get me wrong – they can rub each other up the wrong way, and frankly be really vile to each other (especially Regan inflicting pain on Maxi because . . . well, because she's older and bigger and she can!) but when it comes down to it, they can also be quite sweet together, quite thoughtful of each other's feelings, and Maximus obviously looks up to Regan, so I think he's going to be a bit lost without her.

Brett and Kassie are pretty much absent at the moment. Although I have seen them briefly. So far they're conforming to the media images – Kassie's all bubbly and frothy and Brett's . . . frosty! Mrs E (still mardy, but I manage to keep out of her way most of the time so she's dealable-with) says it's not always like this. To be honest I'm not all that bothered, although there are times when I feel a bit, well, lonely I guess. About the most adult conversation I get in a day is when I do the handovers with Liv and then all we talk about is the kids.

Brett's in the middle of full-on training, it being the beginning of the season. I don't really care whether he's around or not – I actually find him a bit intimidating. I mean, it's bad enough that he looks like some sort of blond god, but the whole mean moody thing? Wouldn't hurt to let a little ray of sunshine into your life every now and again. Actually, that's not entirely fair. The only time I see Brett Ballentine even slightly animated (in a happy way) is around the kids.

He came in the other afternoon and as soon as he walked into the playroom the kids just ran up and bowled him over. Then he did this kind of five-minute rough and tumble on the floor with them laughing hysterically. Finally he pulled himself up and was like: 'Come on, guys, calm down, Daddy's just got to talk to Katie.' And just like that, a switch flicks and the shutters come down.

'Katie, have you got a minute?' He's always very polite, but like I could really say: 'No, bit busy actually, talk to me later.'

'I've got a free afternoon,' he told me. 'So I'll take the kids and you can use the time to get on with something else. OK?'

'Um . . . OK . . . um . . . thanks . . .' I always find myself muttering and tripping over my words when I talk to him. He never says anything horrible, but it's the way he says things. It's like he hates having to even speak to me. As if he'd rather I wasn't there at all.

And then as soon as I'm heading for the door he's back to Superdad mode: 'Come here, you two, give Daddy a hug. Ooooh, I've missed you. Wow! Did you do that Lego . . .' etc. etc.

I'm happy that Brett is so good with the kids but with everyone else, well . . . basically he's just rude. And if you were to ask me if I like him . . . ? So far? Not really. In fact, no.

Kassie on the other hand, she's just the opposite. She is so over-the-top friendly when she's around. The other morning she sort of burst into the playroom, rushed over to me and was instantly gushing: 'Oh, Katie, I'm so sorry I haven't been here much lately.' She gave a little wave at the children, 'Hello, babes . . . But I'm just so tied up with this fitness video and I've got to get on with it now, 'cos after that I've got some stuff with *Hello!* and *Take a Break* lined up and then I'm meant to be getting on with my lingerie range and everything, so if I don't do it now—' Gush gush gush. She is just so manic, that woman, and so open about her life. But I don't care what people say about her – or what her background is. I think the fact that she's trying to make something of herself now is great. And she doesn't talk down to me like Brett does. She talks to me as if I'm an old mate (don't worry, I so know I'm not, but she has a way of making me feel relaxed around her).

And she remembered my birthday – though I think Mrs E reminded her. Mrs E has a list of staff birthdays and efficiency *is* her middle name, along with 'patronising'.

I tell you, she actually talks to Kassie in the same condescending tone she uses for everyone else; I don't know how she gets away with it.

Anyway, Kassie was her usual rush-rush self, but she still found time to come and give me my presents in person.

'Here you go, babes,' she said, handing me a huge parcel and smiling from ear to ear.

I looked a bit hesitant. 'Go on then,' she said, laughing. 'Rip it open!'

I opened the card first, carefully. It was a quite tasteful, arty number. 'Bloody hell, that's a bit posh,' Kassie said (tact not being her middle name). 'You can tell I didn't choose it, can't you, I would have got you something rude!' I had to smile. She is so upfront.

Then I opened the presents. They'd given me this really amazing Louis Vuitton handbag and a voucher for a spa day at Hamston Grange. I couldn't believe it! I was thrilled but sort of embarrassed as well. I mean, it's not like I'm her sister, or even a mate; I'm just the nanny after all. But Kassie seemed genuinely excited for me.

'Hamston Grange is just up the road from our place in Yorkshire,' she explained. 'All the northern-based celebs go there. You'll be rubbing shoulders with a few A-listers there, I tell you. You can have a day off next time we're up there – you deserve it for putting up with these two monkeys.' She patted Maxi, who was lurking round her legs, on the head.

I couldn't help myself. I was so chuffed I lunged at Kassie and gave her a kind of half-hug to say thank you. And then

I thought, oops, crossed the line, but it was OK. She just laughed and said, 'Ah, bless you, Katie, you enjoy it.' How someone that nice and approachable can be married to such a robot, I'll never know.

Hotline magazine – News just in!

Kassie B Fights to Save Marriage!

Kassie Ballentine (23) is fighting to save her two-year marriage after reports that her husband Brett is planning to move out of the family home. According to one source the ex-pole dancer and the Spartacus midfielder aren't on good terms at the moment. 'It's not really working out. The miscarriage was a difficult time for the couple and really exposed some flaws in their relationship'. says a source close to the couple, who went on to say, 'They're trying to work things out and would appreciate some privacy in which to do so.'

5

My first weekend off and I'm at home with my family for my big eighteenth birthday celebration. (I'm celebrating with my mates next time I'm home.) It's quite funny really. Before, everyone was really trying to be cool about me working for the Ballentines and I had several pep talks about not letting it go to my head etc. And then I come home for my birthday, and Mum (who I never thought of as someone who gave a monkey's about the vacuous world of celebrity) apparently has hidden shallows and has invited half of Hastings and every long-lost relative she could dredge up and nobody's even slightly interested in me or how I'm getting on or the fact that it's the big One Eight . . . all they want is the inside info on the family famous.

My Auntie Chelle (Dad's chavvy sister) has been all over me like a rash since I got here. 'I bet that Kassie's a real bitch, isn't she?' Nice opening gambit, Auntie Chelle – don't bother with the 'Happy Birthday', will you?

'Er, no actually, she's really nice.'

'She looks a bit common if you ask me. That picture of her in last week's *Heat* – what *did* she look like?'

This coming from a woman who still insists on wearing a tight, leopard-skin top and leggings despite fast approaching the menopause. I can't talk to Auntie Chelle for long at the best of times. She's a committed chain smoker; being around her for longer than half an hour gives you a good insight into what being a kipper feels like.

'Ohhh, come on, Katie,' she wheedled, changing tack. 'Tell your Auntie Chelle all about it. I bet that Brett walks around in the not-much, eh? I would if I had a body like that!'

'Auntie Chelle! One, no he doesn't and two, I'm not really supposed to discuss the intimate details of my clients' lives. How would you like it if you had someone living with you and they spent their time telling everyone the intimate details of your everyday life?'

Auntie Chelle laughed. 'Wouldn't be much to tell, would there, love. "Uncle Vince in remote-control hand-over shocker!" ' She shrieked with mirth at her own joke. 'That'll really get the tabloids going. Mind you, I've said to our Lynette she could be a Page Three model, she's got a lovely pair she has . . .'

God, that woman is so crass – I can't believe Dad actually grew up in the same house as her, let alone that she's anything to do with Nan. I mean, OK, she's a bit older than Dad but it's like they hatched from completely different eggs. As for poor Lynette, she's twenty-five and still living at home with her hideous mother. She's pretty shy and works in a bank – once again, go figure!

Anyway, when we'd finally managed to get rid of all the liggers and hangers-on I was finally able to have a proper talk with my family.

'What's the house like, love?' my mum asked. 'Your dad said it was an absolute mansion.'

'Well, yeah,' I sighed. There was no way I was going to get to bed tonight if I didn't at least throw them a few scraps. Deep breath in: 'Basically, I've got the top floor – like a major-league attic conversion. And then the children have got the next floor down – with their bedrooms, the playroom, the night nanny's room—'

'Night nanny!' Nan was puce. 'What? Are they too bloomin' posh to get up in the night for their own kids?'

I sighed again. 'It's not about being posh, Nan. They're busy. They've got important stuff to do, they can't be dragging themselves through the day half exhausted because the three-year-old's had a bad dream.'

'Important stuff,' Nan was still indignant. 'What's more important than your own children?'

'Shush, Mum,' my dad cut in. 'Let her finish.'

'So yeah, the night nanny's room – she's called Livvy.' I stared Nan down. 'And a bathroom for the kids. And you should see the rooms. They're all themed and all immaculate – there's a team of cleaners to do them every day. And they've got more books and toys than you'd ever believe.'

'Making up for a lack of love, I'd say,' Nan muttered under her breath.

I ignored her and carried on with my description 'Then

there's a guest room with another en suite and another bathroom which people use if they come for dinner or whatever . . . so they don't have to walk through a bedroom to use the loo!'

'Oooh la la!' my mum laughed. 'You really know you've made it in life when you've got four loos!'

'Six actually,' I said with a grin. 'Mine, the children's, two en suites, one main bathroom and another one downstairs!'

There was a collective snort at how ridiculous it was to have six toilets.

'Do you want me to carry on telling you about the house, or not?' I asked, mock outraged. It was quite nice having an audience hanging on my every word.

They all listened again. 'The next floor has three reception rooms—'

'What, they've got a reception upstairs?' my sister asked.

'No,' my dad said, 'that's just idiot estate-agent speak. It means a living room.'

'What, so they've got three living rooms?' Jo said again.

'Well, yeah,' I answered. 'Actually, five – three on the first floor and two downstairs on the ground floor, along with the kitchen and the dining room, and the annexe has a games room, pool and gym area . . . then there's a really nice garden with climbing stuff and swings for the kids and . . . well, that's about it.'

'As if that's not enough,' Nan sniffed. 'There are people starving in the world and he has all that for kicking a ball around a field . . .'

Even though I had had that thought myself, I ignored her – again. 'Oh yeah, and then there's the other house in Yorkshire, 'cos that's where Brett's from, and the holiday home in Spain . . . and that's about it.'

Jo peered out from beneath her straggly jet-black fringe. 'Wow! Katie, you are *so* lucky!'

'Not as lucky as that Brent Ballentine,' Nan piped up. 'Lucky God gave him such a good right foot, eh? Otherwise he'd be nothing would he. Probably be taking all these drugs and having an ASBO by now!'

That woman has such a talent for putting everything back in perspective!

Close-Up magazine

HE SHOOTS HE SCORES

Brett Ballentine's managed to get one in the back of the net again – with the fantastic news that wife Kassie (23) is expecting a baby in December. The couple, who suffered a miscarriage two years ago, are said to be delighted. A close friend of the couple said, 'It's true they've had their ups and downs, but Brett's a real
family man and there's nothing like a baby to get things back on track.'

6

I got back to London and slipped straight back into work-mode. I've got quite a little routine going now.

Most days I have on my own with Maximus as Regan's at school. Maxi looks a bit like his mum – big brown eyes and sandy hair (the colour I assume hers would be if she kept off the bottle) – whereas Regan takes after Brett, steely blue eyes and white-blonde hair. Regan is five and Maximus is three and half but still hanging on to his status as baby of the family for all it's worth.

We drop Regan off and pick her up though. Sometimes I drive, but if he's available the chauffeur takes us. I have most Wednesdays to myself as Maximus goes to nursery – he needs to start getting used to a structured day before he starts school in September. I use the time to sort their stuff out and do some planning. And then at weekends (the ones I'm working) I usually try to find nice things to do with the kids, which can be a bit tricky as anywhere involving Joe Public and I'm obliged to take a bodyguard with me – can you imagine? So I have to arrange with Ted (kids' bodyguard) before doing anything too adventurous. That's a bit freaky in itself as Ted's about forty, and typical bodyguard material: huge, square and bald. And to say he's the strong silent type doesn't even cover it – the man barely says a word.

But, bodyguards aside, on the whole looking after the kids is great. Maximus is really sweet, very imaginative and dramatic, whereas Regan is much more straightforward, very keen for adult approval and to be a big girl. She's a total tomboy – much to Kassie's disgust. Kassie turned up in the playroom the other day with this huge bag from Rainbow, this kids' designer store. Then she called Regan over – and you could tell from the child's face she was already dreading opening the bag.

'Look darlin',' Kassie trilled, 'Mummy's bought you a lovely pressie.'

Regan reluctantly started pulling things out of the bag. First out was this really hideous strappy little dress which would have looked slutty on an adult let alone a child, and then that was closely followed by a pair of really high wedgy shoes (hello! She's five). Anyone who knows Regan would know that is so *not* what she would want to wear – which speaks volumes about Kassie and her kids, I suppose. She's just too busy, you see.

'Come on then,' Kassie encouraged. 'Try them on, honey.'

Regan looked so unimpressed. 'Do I have to?' she asked. 'I'm just in the middle of a game.' She tilted her head towards the computer in the corner of the room.

'This is much more fun than any silly old game,' Kassie said, and you could tell from her tone she wasn't going to take no for an answer.

I mean, I could see her point. She's bought her daughter a load of presents and Regan's not even slightly interested, let alone grateful. But if she'd asked Regan what she wanted, it would've been a computer game or some complicated Lego set, not some frou-frou frock and a pair of ankle breakers.

And then, after she'd forced Regan into this beauty-pageant outfit, Kassie made her sit down so that she could do her hair and make-up. Poor Regan just looked miserable. She really craves her mother's attention, but then when she gets it, it seems to involve doing something that makes her really uncomfortable.

'Ooooh, doesn't she look fantastic!' Kassie said, standing back and admiring her handiwork. 'Come on then, give us a twirl.'

Regan awkwardly turned on the spot and tried to smile for her mother. Then Maxi chirped up: 'Regan looks horrible, Mummy.' Regan launched herself at him, and beauty-pageant princess turned into all-in wrestling champ in the blink of a beautifully made-up eye.

Apparently Regan and Maxi used to fight with each other quite a bit, but since Regan has started school and they aren't spending quite so much time together they get on a bit better. Poor things. I know they can have everything money can buy, but I'm starting to wonder if it's right that they spend more time with me than they do with their parents.

Parenting skills aside, you've got to admire Kassie in a way. She knows how her image comes across but she doesn't seem to care. Nice but dim, that's the impression the media give of her. Big boobs, hair extensions, stuck-on nails. Main topics of conversation: herself, shopping, which designer labels she'll be sporting to which celebrity do and . . . herself again. But she can be sharp as a tack, funny and bitchy and just plain outrageous, which I find strangely endearing. And she doesn't want to just be the little wifey on Brett's arm for the rest of her life; she wants to be taken seriously in her own right. I don't think there's anything wrong with that. And she takes a lot of flack from the press. She's trying to get her career together and decide what she wants to do, which isn't that easy when her past CV only extends as far as wrapping herself provocatively round a pole and pulling the most eligible bachelor ever.

Oh, yeah, I forgot: she also does a lot of work for charity!

The only thing about her that gets me is how she is with the kids . . . like not that interested. Although maybe that's only when I'm around? I guess when I'm there she sees it as her time, maybe that's why she seems a bit dismissive of them, and then thinks she can buy their affection by turning up with armfuls of stuff – but as she seems completely clueless as to what they actually like, even that's a bit of a waste of time.

* * *

Hmmm. It's not like Kassie's *never* there, but when she is she's kind of preoccupied. She's got so many projects on the go: fitness video, designer underwear range, Kassie B personal grooming products . . .

Sometimes, if we're lucky she'll come and sit up in the playroom with us. She'll bring her coffee and her gossipy mags (she gets them all delivered to the house – never misses a copy) and she pores over them.

I'll be chasing Regan round the room or wiping Maxi's nose and she'll be all: 'Hey, Katie, come and have a look at this. What does she think she looks like?' I try to make out like I'm not that interested – keep that air of professionalism they were always banging on about at college. But I have to admit it is kind of fascinating – she knows some incredible people. I don't mean because they're friends or anything, but they're people who all get invited to the same parties: movie premieres, product launches . . . the opening of an envelope. But Kassie can be really harsh when it comes to dishing out criticism. 'God, look at her, she's piled it on! She is sooooo fat, lard-arsed cow, she's disgusting. Honestly, Katie, if I had cellulite like that, I'd flippin' kill myself – I'm not kiddin'. I saw her at the Stella McCartney show for London Fashion Week – and I swear she was making herself sick in the toilets. And if she wasn't, she bloody well should have been!'

I can't help myself, I always look a bit shocked when she comes out with her little gems. 'Swear to God, Katie, and . . .' pause for effect . . . 'that runny nose she's always got ain't from sniffing Vicks – know what I mean?'

41

And if it's a picture of her she can go on about it for hours. 'I've gone off that dress, it makes me look a bit fat, don't you think? Jesus, even my arms look fat! Mind you, it's the angle, innit. They're bastards them photographers.' She's absolutely not bothered about the kids being around – she'll say anything that pops into her mind. 'I've gone off that slashed look anyway, ever since that Rosie Rotherham started wearing it. 'She's sort of cheapened it, know what I mean?' (she can really stick the knife into other WAGS).

Then I'll try desperately to say the right thing. I mean, Kassie is like a walking bag of boney bling! 'Well, perhaps with different accessories . . .'

'Mmmm, yeah, maybe. And I might try a different make-up artist next time – I don't think that one really got the Kassie B "look". And she was a stuck-up cow. I tell you, some people think they're better than me . . .' She paused for a moment, lost in thought, then . . . 'Still, I dunno about that dress. Anyway, it's not like I'd wear it again, it only cost me three grand. You can have it if you like.'

Seriously!

And I'm doing a reasonable impression of an idiot, trying to politely decline her offer without actually pointing out that firstly, I wouldn't be seen dead in any of the scraps of cloth she calls clothing and secondly, even if I were to share her somewhat 'eccentric' taste, I certainly don't share her dress-size. She is TINY. Like real micro-woman. I don't think I'd even fit my thigh in her waistband.

Every now and again one of the children will satellite

round to her and try to get her to come and play. And she's incredible – she doesn't even look up from her magazine, she just lights another cigarette (yes – in the playroom!) and says: 'Not now, darlin', Mummy's really busy . . .'

The thing is, I know enough about Maximus and Regan by now to tell when they're hungry or tired or worried about something. I can anticipate what they might want to do – when they need to let off steam, when they need quiet time – and I structure the day around them and their needs. And I can see that when Mummy can't even be bothered to talk to them it hurts their little feelings and, to be honest, it upsets me too.

But then the other day Kassie and me had a bit of a heart-to-heart (well, I say heart-to-heart, but it was more her talking and me listening) and I actually felt a bit sorry for her.

'Did you have a nice birthday?' she asked me. 'Did you see your family and that?'

I nodded. 'Mmm, yes thanks, we had a bit of a party, you know.' I didn't go into detail. I'm sure Kassie's idea of a party is a bit different to sitting in my mum's kitchen eating vol-au-vents and listening to Nan's varicose-vein sagas.

'That's nice,' she said. 'My eighteenth was really crap. I was living in this complete dive with this guy who was a total using arsehole. I'd already lived away from home for three years by that time.' She sighed. 'My family were totally useless.'

I stared at her. I vaguely remembered reading something

about her mum having a drink problem. I know Kassie's an open person but I hadn't expected her to be quite so frank about it.

'My mum was on the piss for most of my life. Can't really remember her ever being sober.' She smiled ruefully. 'And as for my stepdad . . . I tell you what, Katie, that man can rot in hell for all I care. Violent bastard. You know, he turned up out the woodwork a few years ago. Thought he'd make a quid or two now that I've come good. "Come on, Kassie, let's bury the hatchet," he said. "The only place I'd bury the hatchet is in your head!" I told him. So then he does this sob-story exclusive for the *News of the World*. I tell you what, I couldn't even be bothered to respond – he'll get what's coming to him. Still, I suppose I grew up fast – know how to take care of myself. And there's something to be said for that, I reckon.'

'Do you see your mum now?' I asked. I felt a bit shocked to be honest. I know my own family drive me mad sometimes, but at least they're more or less normal, and they're always there for me.

'My mum's dead,' Kassie said sharply. She crushed her cigarette with a bit more force than was necessary into the ashtray.

We sat in silence for a moment. I struggled to say something that wasn't a total cliché.

'Kassie, I didn't realize . . .' I began lamely.

'No point crying over spilt milk,' Kassie cut in, a touch too brightly. She pulled one of her top-model smiles out of the bag. 'I may have had a shit start in life, but I'm doing OK now, aren't I?'

That's another reason why I like Kassie. Self-pity isn't her thing. She just gets on with it. OK, she's never going to win Mother of the Year, but then an alcoholic mother and a violent step-dad aren't exactly the best role models.

Close-Up (2002)

What a pleasant surprise to see Kassie Ballentine looking almost understated(!) as she showed off her baby bump at the prestigious British Book Awards at London's Grosvenor House Hotel. Perhaps the thought of being a mum's brought a new level of maturity to the ex-glamour girl . . . but we doubt it!

7

'Carly!'

'Katie, hi! How's it going?'

'Brilliant! How are you?' I tucked the phone under my chin and reached for an emery board.

'Knackered. Diane's got this new Indian head massage training initiative thingy going on, so we're all staying late every evening to practise. And then I've got a study day for colouring techniques at the college on Saturday – I love slapping on the chemicals and that, but I'm not going to be able to squeeze in a big Friday night out for a while – I'm well hacked off.'

Carly loves her job but finds her boss Diane a bit of a nightmare control freak. In short, Carly can't stand her. She's always on the look-out for a new job, so she says, but so far nothing's come of it. I keep trying to persuade her to move to London. I know she'd love it – for the shopping alone. As I said, Carly's much more fashionista than me and she says that living at home means she's got the spare cash to keep her gear cutting edge. These days she keeps wittering on about not being able to afford to move to

London and 'not everyone can live the life of a millionaire princess . . .' I can't think what she means!

'Anyway, how about you?' she asked. 'Your life has to be more interesting than mine, surely!'

'Well, there was sports day at Regan's school today, and Brett and Kassie took part in the parents' races which, in Brett's case, was a bit unfair on the other parents.'

'God, I'll say – some fat middle-aged stockbroker up against the country's fittest male. And I should think Kassie had to keep hold of her boobs – in case she put someone's eye out,' Carly laughed.

'Ahhh, it was quite sweet though,' I smiled. 'Regan was so chuffed. You could just tell it made her day, her mum and dad both there for her. I mean, it's a really small and exclusive school, about a hundred kids and all filthy rich, so it's not like anyone was really fazed by Brett and Kassie being there – and if they were, they had enough breeding not to show it! And Kassie put on a good show, talking to all the kids and everything. And every time there was a photographer there she gathered them all together for the shot. Which did look pretty bizarre as her and Brett were in matching sportswear! Kassie's idea, of course. But even Brett managed to raise the odd smile.'

'What did you do then?'

'Well, I had Maxi most of the time. He got so excited when his mum and dad's races were on, too. He's so funny, he was going: "Run Daddy, run like a pig!"'

Carly laughed. 'He's mad as a stick, that one!'

47

'Oh yeah, and I met Kassie's manager as well.'

'Let me guess. Not very nice?'

God, Carly could read me like a book. 'Let's just say, he's called Ken and I've already added "Creepy" to the front.'

'That nice, eh?' Carly laughed.

'Really smarmy. Apparently him and Kassie had some bust-up a while ago and she was looking around for another manager but somehow they've managed to kiss and make up. Ew! It makes my skin crawl just thinking about it. I tell you, he's like this total throwback. He actually slaps her on the arse when she walks past and says: "All right, baby," and then she giggles hysterically. It's totally gross.'

'Are you sure you're not jealous, darling?' Carly joked.

'Don't even go there.' I grimaced at the thought of Creepy Ken with his wide-boy suits and naff jewellery. He was a joke. Why Kassie bothers with him I can't imagine. 'Even Mrs E seems to defrost a bit when he's there,' I paused. 'But then, she is more in his age bracket . . . and maybe the thought of all that money . . .'

'Well . . .' Carly paused. 'If he's minted I might go for him myself. I tell you, even with the odd hefty tip it's not enough. Diane's driving me mad. I've gotta get out of there. Go on, Katie, give us Creepy Ken's number. He can't be any worse than some of the losers I've snogged round here!'

Hmm. I think she was joking, but you never can tell with Carls.

Carly paused for a beat. 'Speaking of losers . . .' I could

almost feel her sense of hesitation down the phone. '. . . I saw Josh the other night.'

I ignored the dig. Carly couldn't help herself when it came to Josh. I bit my lip. Don't blurt, I thought to myself. 'Oh, really,' I said, trying desperately to sound calm. Why is it that even the mention of his name still has this stupid effect on me?

'Yeah, he was asking after you.'

'Oh,' I said. I so wanted to grill her but I so knew what her response would be.

It was like she read my mind. 'You're not still interested in him, Katie, are you?' she said, disbelief in her voice. 'Not after the way he treated you?'

'Well, no . . . but . . .' I floundered. 'Well, it's just, you know, we were together a long time. I can't just forget that.'

'Hmmm.' Carly sounded less than impressed.

'So come on, what did he say about me?' I couldn't help myself.

Carly sighed down the phone. 'Oh you know, the usual, asked what you were up to and that . . .' She paused again. 'He wanted to know if you still had the same phone number and email address.'

My heart skipped a beat.

'You don't seriously want him to get back in touch with you, do you?' Carly asked. 'The guy was a complete bastard.'

'I know,' I wheedled, 'but just talking to him wouldn't do any harm, would it?'

Carly snorted down the phone. 'Look, Katie, it's your life,

but don't come crying to me when he turns out to be just as much of a rat as he always was.'

'Honestly, Carly. He may never get in touch. He was probably just making conversation . . .' Was he just making conversation? I wished I didn't care but I could already feel the oh-so-familiar 'Josh Butterflies' fluttering in my tummy.

'Yeah, well, let's hope so,' Carly said. 'I really don't want to see you getting hurt like that again, Katie.'

I know, I thought. And I don't want that either.

Hotline magazine

AND BABY B MAKES THREE

Proud parents Brett and Kassie Ballentine couldn't wait to show off the newest addition to their family. The Spartacus FC striker (23) and Kassie (23) happily posed for photographs with newborn daughter, Regan, outside the exclusive Portman Hospital in London as they prepared to take her home.

Brett, looking uncharacteristically cheerful, said, 'I'm on top of the world. I'm so overjoyed – just the most amazing feeling – I can't believe I have a daughter.'

Daughter Regan weighed 7lb and was delivered by planned Caesarian section last Wednesday.

Brett seemed overcome as he declared that his new daughter is the spitting image of him. 'Yes, I suppose she does look a bit like me – but whatever, she's absolutely gorgeous.'

8

Weird day today. I was with the kids in the playroom. I'd picked up Regan from school – did I mention the car that comes with the job? A gorgeous little red Mini Cooper (not so cool with Maxi's child seat in the back though!). Good job I finally passed my test at the beginning of the summer (fifth time lucky, that's what I always say). Although the first few times I drove in London I was absolutely terrified. My teeth were clenched so tightly you almost had to prise my mouth open at the end of the journey. Luckily there's also the use of a chauffeur-driven vehicle available for most of the time with the kids – but unfortunately not today.

Regan was quite tired after school so I let her watch a DVD. And I'd got all the Play-Doh out for Maxi and we were making 'worms' and 'eggs'.

'My worm is actually a snake,' Maxi told me. 'He is red and he eats slug sandwiches.'

Funny kid.

Anyway, Kassie came in, fags and mags in hand, and she goes and sits next to Regan to watch the telly – well, smoke and read. But at least she was with her. I could see how happy it made Regan feel just to have her mummy there. Kassie even put her arm around Regan for a few minutes – until the need to have another cigarette necessitated her getting her arm back.

Didn't last long, of course. Kassie started pacing the room with her mobile. She sent about a zillion text messages and had a phone call with Creepy Ken: 'Oh, Kenny, you're not cross with ickle Kassie, are you . . . ?' Cringe-making.

In the meantime Maxi was beginning to tire of Play-Doh and his hands were so caked in the stuff that he could barely flex his fingers.

'I'm just taking Maximus to wash his hands,' I called over to Regan and Kassie. Two blond heads bobbed in acknowledgement.

'Come on then, Maxi. Don't touch anything on the way,' I warned. Expensive ivory paint and silk drapes all over that particular landing – just perfect when there are two small children around – not!

Maxi took quite a while in the bathroom. He's not the speediest of kids at the best of times but after we'd washed his hands he couldn't make up his mind if he needed a poo or not. So, it was another five minutes deciding, a few minutes trying, a couple of minutes doing, a few more minutes discussing (why little children like to talk about their business so much I'll never know) and then another few minutes persuading him that yes he did need to wash his hands again even though he'd just done it before etc. etc. before we could get him dried up, tucked in and back on his way to the playroom.

I think I can be a bit dim sometimes. You see, I heard the voices way before we'd crossed the landing. But for some reason I assumed that it was Regan's DVD. Er, yeah, Katie, remember that scene where the Aristocats are at each others' throats?

I was already at the door before I fully realized what was going on. Brett was now in the playroom with Kassie and they were having a full-blown row. Granted they weren't really shouting, more sort of hissing at each other – but nevertheless it was obvious to anyone over the age of five (hopefully) that they weren't best pleased with each other.

'Can't you survive without a fag for five minutes?' – Brett.

'The window's open, sweetie, and Regan doesn't mind, do you, darlin'?' Kassie said.

'Regan, darling,' Brett said, obviously trying to keep his tone light. 'Go and find Nanny Katie while me and your mum have a chat.'

A few seconds later Regan came out of the door to find Maxi and me looking awkward in the corridor. 'Shhh,' I said.

She didn't make a sound. Just came up and held my hand. Brett's voice continued behind the playroom door.

'Of course Regan's not going to say she minds, she's probably so overwhelmed by the fact that you're actually paying her any attention at all—' He stopped abruptly. 'What the hell is that on your arm?'

'Oh, what, this . . . ?'

Maximus suddenly recognized his father's voice and started going for the door. 'Daddy! My daddy's home!'

I didn't know what to do. I could feel panic rising, I didn't want to walk into the middle of a domestic, but I had an overexcited three-year-old tugging my arm out of the socket trying to make a break for it.

'How about we surprise Daddy?' I said to both kids. 'Let's hide and when he's stopped talking to Mummy we can jump out!'

They looked a little uncertain at first but then Maxi's face lit up in a smile. 'OK! I'm going under the table,' he whispered, while Regan just shrugged. Poor little mite. I'd actually meant going to hide in another room, but Maximus was off under the table before I could stop him.

Maxi, Regan and I crouched down under the little landing table. I was much too big to fit under there but I'd made the stupid suggestion and I felt I had to follow through.

'Kabbalah!' I could hear Brett's scathing tones. 'Since when did you think you were Madonna?'

'Since Thursday.' Nothing, it seemed, rattled Kassie.

'Thursday! What, so you've been deeply spiritual for four days?'

'Something like that, yeah. Let's face it, if it's good enough for Madge . . .'

'Yeah, but she's probably taking it seriously, Kassie. You don't just wear the thread and that's it – you've got to read stuff, attend meetings!'

'I read stuff!' Kassie countered.

Maxi was fidgeting beside me. 'When's my daddy coming out?' Regan just looked miserable.

'Really soon,' I whispered. 'Shhhhh, or he'll find us!'

'Yeah, I didn't actually mean *Closer* magazine. For God's sake, Kassie, you're as shallow as a puddle. You'll be adopting yourself an accessory baby next, just to get your face in the papers.'

'I resent that, Brett. Just because I haven't embraced my spiritual side before doesn't mean I haven't got one. My psychic astrologer told me I would find new layers of karmic mysticism within myself—'

Brett cut her short. 'Jesus! What a load of rubbish!'

No reply, then little-girl-lost voice. 'I don't know why you can't just be happy that I've found something so life-affirming to enrich my being with . . .'

Brett was quiet. I strained my ears trying to work out what was happening. But, by the time I'd realized that on the other side of the door he'd turned on his heel and was about to join us on the landing, Maxi was already leaping up and out from under our hiding place.

'Surprise!' he yelled, jumping up towards his dad.

And as I, the table, and the huge vase on top of it toppled over, I caught the steely glint in Brett's eye and knew that he wasn't very impressed.

OK, so I'd made a mistake. But where am I supposed to go with the kids if he's picking a fight with his wife in their playroom?

But that's Brett for you. Still, Regan and Maxi just luuuurrrrve their daddy. Them and half the nation! But not . . . me.

Close-Up magazine

Cake it on Kassie

Why oh why does Kassie Ballentine cover up her pretty face with panstick, a whole kohl pencil, a pot of bronzer and dreadful lip liner? It makes her look like a clown! Surely a tinted moisturiser, nude lip gloss and shimmery shadow would make her look far sexier.

9

I took Regan and Maxi to a city farm this morning (Ted came too) and they just loved it. Ted's not so bad and he can be quite helpful with the kids. And I'm beginning to get used to it, as I guess if anything ever did kick off I'd certainly be grateful for having Ted around. Plus, he's happy to drive which means I don't have to do the London Traffic Terror Ride.

At first I was really quite nervous about taking the kids out on my own. It's always strange having responsibility for other people's children when you're out and about. It's suddenly like danger lurks all around: busy roads, crowded cafés, weirdo people. I'm constantly imagining I've lost one of them and having several mini heart attacks before realizing they're standing right next to me. To begin with I also felt a bit freaked that people would recognize the kids, but so far that hasn't really happened.

It's not as if they haven't been photographed like a zillion times, but when it's a pap shot their faces are pixilated anyway, so they go all fuzzy and you can't really see them. So it's only on officially sanctioned shots that you actually get to see them clearly. And then I think people don't really recognize them out of context. Maybe they just assume they're mine and Ted's – now that really is a weird concept! Regan's the spitting image of her father, so it's also a pretty unlikely concept. Ted's quite sweet, but boy-babe he ain't. Plus he's just about old enough to be my dad!

We went on a tractor ride over to where they keep the horses. Regan was really sweet talking to the ponies, she was tickling their ears and saying, 'Ooh darlin', you all right, sweetheart?' in this slightly Cockney twang – guess she gets that from her mum.

After that we went and had some lunch in the café. And then a waiter brought it over for us and the children both said 'Thank you' without being prompted. And Regan said, 'Excuse me, could I have some ketchup, please' and then, 'Thank you' again when the waiter brought it. And when he came to clear the table the waiter said to me and Ted, 'Your children are so polite.' I couldn't have felt prouder if they *were* my children – and I could tell Ted felt the same. We shared this little proud glance with each other and if I didn't know better I'd have sworn he was welling up!

Once we got home the kids were looking pretty worn out – we'd done the playground and the pigsties and the little furry animal petting area after lunch – so we quickly made some popcorn in the kitchen and then I let them choose a DVD to watch.

When the film had finished we got out the paints and the

glue and the craft stuff and despite it being the middle of October the kids made cotton-wool snowmen pictures. Then we had dinner all together in the kitchen. The chef hasn't got much on at the moment as Kassie is on the 'juicer' diet. So she only eats (or should that be drinks?) pureed fruit and veg in the day and then has a bit of grilled fish and steamed vegetables for dinner, while Brett is on some high-protein, low-fat training diet, so Ricardo is quite happy to cook for us. Tonight it was his world-famous meatballs (his description not mine) with freshly prepared pasta. The children call them footballs rather than meatballs and Regan spends the whole mealtime doing a football commentary at the same time. Ricardo is really sweet with the kids too. It's nice, because they may not see much of their parents but they are surrounded by people who seem to really care about them – and not in a sucky-uppy kind of way. Perhaps everyone feels just a little bit sorry for them. Ironic, considering how 'lucky' they are in so many ways. Money, security, A-list parents . . . What more could a kid want?

BRETT AND KASSIE ARE BACK ON THE BALL

If this doesn't put paid to rumours about their marriage being on the rocks, nothing will. Kassie Ballentine and striker husband Brett were spotted kissing in the spring sunshine on a trip to New York. Kassie (24) and Brett (24) were shopping in the city's SoHo district. Stories that all wasn't well between the couple had circulated after Kassie had lost their first baby but it seems since their new baby Regan (6 months) has come along they couldn't be closer. Kassie had blamed Brett's punishing schedule for the strain on their marriage but it seems that when they do get time together, they certainly make the most of it.

11

To: carlymurphy@spscarechild.com
From: kmeredith@eggspok.com
Subject: Helloooo!

Amazing news of the week – if there can be anything more amazing than just having this freaky job! Kassie's got *Hello!* magazine coming round to do a spread and she wants me there to lend a hand and maybe be in a picture! I'm soooo nervous!
More soon – gotta dash and do some beautifying to look my best for the camera!
xxx
Katie

Home this weekend, hurrah! I made Mum promise that Auntie Chelle would be banned from the premises. Pretty easy really – Mum just 'forgot' to tell her I was coming home, and as the woman's usually not in the slightest bit interested in what any of us are up to, it's not like she'd be dropping by on the off chance.

I dumped my bag on the bed in my room, which seemed so tiny compared to my spacious 'suite' of rooms back in London. Tiny, and childish. My poster of S Club 7 is still there and I can even see a pair of Barbie's legs sticking out next to the bookshelf. It's all so familiar and yet it all feels as if it belongs to another Katie, one from another time, which, in a way, I suppose it does. I haven't properly lived at home for ages – I was only fifteen when I left school (youngest in my year) and then I'd just turned sixteen when I went off to do my training in London. I think Mum and Dad found it hard to let me go, but they knew what a tough time I was having over the whole Jush thing. So they arranged for me to stay with some old friends of theirs whose daughter was away at uni so it all worked out quite well really. Maybe that's why I have this strange empathy with Kassie. We both left home and made our way out into the big wide world when we were teenagers. Obviously, the similarity stops there. I always knew I had something to come back to if and when I needed it. Even moving away from home, they made sure I'd be really looked after under the watchful eye of Auntie Jackie and Uncle Dave! And even when I spent most of my holidays working abroad, we were never out of touch – Mum even went on a computer course to learn the finer points of emailing.

It's kind of sweet how my mum keeps my room the same. I mean, she must change the bedding and everything between my visits but she always puts all my old cuddly toys back on the end of the bed in exactly the same order they've always been in. You could fit our house three times into the Ballentines' – it's small, but it's home.

It's nice to actually sit down for a family meal, too. Usually in London it's just me, or me and the kids, and very occasionally Brett. But Kassie doesn't actually eat so it's akin to torture for her to be around the kids' leftovers around teatime. She sometimes stands over by the noticeboard, fag in hand, gazing like a hungry vulture at Regan's uneaten beans on toast, but mostly she keeps herself a safe distance from anything other than green tea and rice cakes.

That's not to say it's all peace and love in the Meredith house. Nan's still grumbling about the price of fish when she's round. And this weekend Jo did her usual 'I'm a vegetarian and I don't want my spuds cooked in animal fat' speech. Funny how she bends the rules a bit when it comes to bacon sandwiches. And Oli, well, he's as pesky and oblivious as ever. Usually, he just tunes out of the family disputes, with his iPod earplugs wedged in position, or he and Dad talk over the females about football results, but this time he asked me a million questions about Brett and Spartacus, none of which I could answer as my brain simply refuses to absorb any information at all concerning football. Mum tried her best to keep everyone grounded, and to steer the conversation away from luxury townhouses and servants and *Hello!* magazine gossip, but it's a bit like sticking an elephant in a room full of humans. Even if you don't talk about it, it's there, getting in everyone's way.

* * *

After dinner on Saturday Carly came round – of course. We were going to get ready together for a night on the town, my belated eighteenth bash. Carly had phoned a couple of mates from school and we were hitting all the old haunts. Carly lent me her skinniest skinny jeans and one of her cute little boho tops. She straightened my hair to within an inch of its life so that it hung gorgeously, like a sleek blonde curtain framing my face. I love it when Carly works her magic on me!

The thing about old haunts is that they usually come with old mates. Great, if they are old mates you want to bump into. But not if you're trying to avoid your lying cheat of an ex-boyfriend.

I went to get the first round of drinks in, and fought my way successfully to the bar to get served. I was just loading up a tray with God knows how many bottles of Smirnoff Ice to take back to our table, when I felt this gentle tap on my shoulder. Now, call it sixth sense, but I would have known that tap anywhere.

A hundred emotions ran through me before I even had time to turn around. I so want to be over him, and in lots of ways I am, but being in the same room as him and being about two inches away from him is a different story.

At least I'd had the Carly treatment before coming out. If I was going to have to bump into Josh, thank God I was looking my most gorgeous.

'Hello, stranger,' he said softly, and then he smiled and I

remembered why I had been so utterly and completely in love with Josh Markham for so long.

'Hi.' I picked up the tray and reversed slightly away from the bar, trying my very best to create an air of busy-can't-talk-right-now. But Josh wasn't taking the hint.

'I hear you live in London now.' He pushed his fingers through his tousled hair, which did nothing for my resolve. 'Working for Brett Ballentine, is it?' He looked down at my hands clutching the tray. 'Can I help you with that?'

I glanced over at Carly, who was scowling like a fishwife in the background. 'I'm fine, thanks,' I said. 'The job's great. Everything's great.' I edged round Josh. 'I couldn't be happier, actually.'

'Good,' Josh said firmly. 'We really should meet up then. I'm working in London a lot these days.'

I was all too aware of Carly's eyes boring into the back of me like a magnetic beam, trying to pull me back to the table. In a way I wished she'd just leave me to it. I know she hated him for how he'd treated me and I guess she really didn't want me to be hurt again. But there was no chance of that. I was in full control of the situation.

'Yeah,' I said. 'Well, maybe . . . Who are you working for, then?' I shouted in an undignified manner over the noise of the bar.

'You know Carstons? The contractors based down here?' I nodded; they were a local firm. 'Well, they've got me doing the electrics for an office round Waterloo. Money's pretty good. Gets a bit lonely, though . . .' And then he gave me this ridiculously charming puppy-dog look. 'I'm Billy No-mates these days . . .'

I felt my face go hot. I couldn't help it. Thank God it was dark in there. 'Oh really?' I said. 'You've always got Megan though, haven't you. She loves to keep the boys company, from what I've heard.' Oh dear, that was totally transparently sour grapes talking. I tried to plaster a good-natured smile on my face to compensate.

Josh didn't bat an eyelid, just continued to stare at me with his big brown eyes. 'I'm not really seeing her any more,' he said calmly. Why did his lashes have to be so long, damn him?

I think maybe I started to move my mouth, but I'm pretty sure no words came out.

'Katie?' Carly's voice cut through the hubbub. 'Need a hand?' She gave Josh a spectacularly icy look. 'With the drinks, that is.'

'Er, great, yeah, thanks . . .' I stammered. 'Bye, Josh.' I managed to sound calmer than I felt. 'See you around.' I turned and grabbed two of the bottles and followed Carly's retreating back through the crowd. I had to get away from him. Being in his presence had a seriously bad effect on me. I didn't swoon at his feet, but he still had the power to get my heart racing, dammit. Josh was dangerous, and I was supposed to be making a fresh start without him in my life. But I couldn't help feeling just the teeniest bit triumphant that he and Megan had finished. Who dumped who? I wondered.

After the Josh blip, the evening turned out to be just what I needed. Being out with the old crowd made me realize how isolated I sometimes feel in London. The kids are great. When I'm on my own with them I'm probably at my most relaxed. It's just living in that house where I am constantly walking on eggshells, terrified of touching anything, spending my weeks with a bunch of people who I'm not so comfortable with. People whose lives are just surreal. Kassie and Brett treat me well, but they're my employers, not my friends. Even Kassie, with her earthy directness, has that steely look in her eye – the look that says, 'Don't come too close, don't push it, girl'. I know my place all right.

Carly and I ended up drinking a little too much, and dancing like we had in the old days. At midnight we teetered home, stopping off at the chippie on the way. As we sat on the wall outside my house, wolfing down chips and gossiping, it felt like I'd never left. I was ordinary old Katie again. It felt all comforting and good. And I didn't even think about Josh Markham. Not much, anyway.

On Sunday, Nan came round again for lunch. Since Gramps died she spends a lot of time round my mum and dad's. She's a funny old stick – all cantankerous and gruff on the outside, but everyone knows that underneath she's just an old softie. She'd help anyone, would Nan. When I was little, she looked after us a lot of the time when Mum was working and I used to absolutely love it. She just always seemed to have so much time for me and would take an interest in whatever I was doing. Seems things haven't changed.

'So, how you enjoying that new job then, Katie?' she asked. 'I've seen pictures of those little 'uns – they look like lovely children.'

'They are, Nan,' I said. And I settled down to tell her about some of the classic things they come out with. Ooh, it made a nice change talking about what I actually do for a living, rather than answering questions about what Kassie looks like first thing in the morning, or if Brett wears Y-fronts or boxers! Nan's not interested in 'tittle tattle' (her words, not mine).

'I took them to one of the city farms,' I said. 'Ahh, you should have seen them, Nan. They loved it.'

'You take them on your own then, did you?' Nan asked.

'Well, me and their minder, Ted.' I could see as soon as the word 'minder' left my lips that Nan was not going to approve.

'Minder! Poor little buggers. Why can't their mum and dad "mind" them, then?'

'Well,' I said, taking a deep breath. Nan's very old-fashioned on some fronts and 'family – the demise of' is one of her favourite topics. 'Brett Ballentine tends to be a bit busy a lot of the time. Y'know, training and ... er ... playing football.'

'Hmmmph!' Nan didn't give two hoots about that, obviously. 'And the mother? That Kassie woman, where was she?'

'Probably charity work,' I fibbed, knowing that telling Nan Kassie had gone shopping would probably push her right over the edge of reason and into rant mode. 'She's really busy, she's got loads on . . .' I could hear how hollow my words sounded as I was saying them. Kassie paid me to hang out with her kids for the day so that she didn't have to. I knew that would be my nan's way of looking at it, and I've got to admit, she did have a point.

Sunday Weekly

KASSIE B SNUBBED FOR PAGE 3 FAVOURITE!

Kassie Ballentine didn't exactly behave like a coy young mum when she heard arch-rival, glamour model Vixen, had beaten her to a lucrative make-up contract. When she realized her nemesis had clinched the £200,000 endorsement she got straight on the blower and gave the company concerned an ear-singeing mouthful. Ouch!

11

Well, we've had the *Hello!* team here for the day and I have to admit, in spite of the fact that we had great stretches of time sitting around, it was just a tiny bit exciting. I mean, me? In *Hello!*? Getting my hair and make-up done by a professional! Fantastic.

Apparently there's going to be this 'Introducing the Ballentines' new nanny' bit, which I must admit I can't wait to see. Carly is going to just die. I mean, I think I'm only going to be in the background and stuff and probably really small – but, hello? *Hello!*

So anyway, we were all primped and preened. Kassie had got it into her head that I should look like a 'proper' nanny and so she got me up in this ridiculous old-fashioned outfit. That did take a bit of the shine off the day. My one chance of sharing in the super-glam lifestyle and instead I'd gone all frumpy super-nanny. Still, I took consolation in the amazing up-do that the hairdresser created for me, held in place with so much hairspray that I thought I might have to invest in some industrial-strength shampoo to get the stuff out again.

Brett and Kassie and the kids were all wearing outfit

number one: the formal evening look. Poor little Regan had been forced into this hideous designer frock and shoes with heels. Maxi had been stuffed into this mini-Brett designer suit and his hair was all fluffed and tousled and sprayed. And then they were all arranged in this really unnatural 'natural' pose, like they always spend their evenings with Kassie lying on a chaise longue, wearing a ball gown, the rest of the family draped artistically around her. And then the camera guy took a Polaroid which they all had to look at (actually Brett wasn't that interested, but Kassie was like scrutinising it for the tiniest detail before she'd let them take the actual shot). Or they were saying things like, 'No, too dark, we have to adjust the lights again,' or the folds in her dress weren't quite right or a strand of hair had come loose . . . and all of this took about an hour. And *then* it had to be done all over again for another four outfits, and each time it was the same procedure. Change of room, set everything up again, change of clothes, hair, make-up, pose, Polaroid, adjustments, pose again, shot . . . The poor kids were just so bored they didn't know what to do with themselves, and Kassie didn't really help matters – she'd brought this bumper bag of sweeties and every time one of them got whingey she'd bribe them with a sweet to do as they were told. By the afternoon Regan and Maximus were virtually bouncing off the walls with the sugar-related high.

But there was no way Kassie was letting them off the hook. If she wanted them in a shot, she wanted them in a shot. Brett kept muttering grumpily under his breath and then he actually said he was going to take the kids out to 'let off steam' for half an hour. Kassie wasn't pleased, but at least Brett actually thinks about his kids' welfare occasionally.

I went to go out after them but Brett stopped me in my tracks. 'You stay with Kassie, Katie,' he said.

I hovered in the doorway. I quite fancied getting out of there for a bit. It wasn't exactly an atmosphere of light and love in the house – Kassie was looking daggers at Brett and, for some reason, me too. Then Maximus piped up, 'I want Katie to come with me.' As he was already emotionally a bit on the wobbly side due to the amount of refined sugar coursing through his veins, I think Brett realized now was not the time to argue. So out I went.

It was a bit awkward at first. Brett's obviously used to getting his own way and he's also not really used to sharing his kids. When he has them, he usually has them on their own. But the kids were so full of beans it was hard not to have a good time in the end. Maxi was mad for playing hide-and-seek. But I had to play alongside him as his grasp of the rules is pretty sketchy. Regan or Brett would count and we'd go and hide and I'd have to put my hand over Maxi's mouth to stop him shouting, 'Here I am!' And he kept picking really useless hiding places – behind a very small, spindly rose bush, or on the swing – like, no one can see us here, Maxi! But Brett and Regan were really good and kept playing along with him, saying: 'I haven't seen Maxi and Katie anywhere, have you?' even when they were virtually in front of us. And then Maxi wouldn't be able to contain himself any more and he'd shout, 'We're here! We're here!' and Brett and Regan would go, 'Ohhh wow!' all surprised, 'We didn't see you there, Maxi, what a good hider you are!' and Maxi would nearly explode he was so delighted. Brett really laughed, and it changed his whole face and I realized what it was . . . he actually looked happy. I don't think I'd ever really seen him look like that before.

And then Kassie came out.

She was already in outfit number four (sort of classic, horsey, country casuals – *so* not her) and her hair had been all slicked down. She had this rictus smile fixed on her face and she was virtually spitting between her teeth. 'Perhaps you could come in now, darlin',' she said in this really fake happy-happy, everything's-fine way, while her eyes were like shards of steel. 'We don't want to keep everyone waiting now, do we?'

Brett shook his head in resignation. 'Come on, you two,' he said quietly. 'Your mother needs us for her latest bit of self-promotion.'

Kassie flashed back: 'I heard that, Brett. Not in front of the staff, eh?' The staff obviously being me. Oh God, I just wanted to disappear into a gigantic hole in the ground. 'And Katie,' she snapped, no longer even bothering to pretend that everything was just A-OK, 'the children need to get changed again – and I believe that's what we pay *you* for.'

And before I even had time to reply, she was stomping back up to the house looking like she was about to find some horse and gallop furiously off into the sunset on it.

'What's wrong with Mummy?' Maxi asked, his little face clouded with confusion. 'Is she cross with me?'

'No, darling, of course not,' I reassured him. 'She's just a bit . . . tired. Come on, let's go and get you changed.'

We all trudged miserably back to the house, very much game over. And then Mrs E came in with some refreshments and looked at me like I was something nasty she'd just stepped in and I suddenly felt really stupid and embarrassed, dressed up like a dog's dinner and posing for the camera, like anyone in the world would be interested in me.

Close-Up magazine

KASSIE'S LACY LOVELY

Forget whites or pretty pastels, this week the passion is for purple. Celebrities are starting autumn wearing every shade from lilac to lavender. Get the Kassie Ballentine look without overdoing it – mix with muted olive and coffee tones for the day, then team with gold accessories by night for instant glitz. We love Kassie's lacy lavender number.

12

Kassie is such a pro. As soon as she was back in the house and back in front of all the *Hello!* team, she was back to nice-as-pie mode. She'd stormed up there looking like she was fit to kill someone, then she threw open the French doors and was all: 'Right. How we doing for time? The nanny's just going to pop the children into some clean clothes.' She turned and smiled at me like butter wouldn't melt. 'Why don't you change into something more comfy, Katie? You must be sick of being stuck in that frumpy get-up all day.'

I wasn't sure if she was having a dig or not, but I didn't need any more of an excuse to get me and the kids out of there – pronto!

Kassie can switch from raging bull to sweetness and light in the blink of an eye. Like I say, she's a real pro. I guess it's all that time spent hanging provocatively off a pole and having to look like you fancy the fat, ugly bloke in the front row who keeps shoving tenners down your thong. Not sure I could do it, but I can see how, for Kassie, it was pretty much the ideal career move.

To be fair, from what I've seen of Kassie this week, I think the whole photo-shoot thing was getting to her a bit more then she let on. For me it was a novelty, if hard work, and for the kids it was a chore. But for Kassie – I think it was really important. I mean, she's always in the press but usually in a way she has no control over. But with *Hello!* she calls the shots. So I suppose having a whole magazine team round your house to take pictures of your family draped beautifully around the place only to find that the rest of them have nicked off for an impromptu game of hide and seek must have been pretty annoying.

To: kmeredith@eggspok.com
From: joshsparkym@hotletters.com
Re: Long time no email

Hi Katie
Just wanted to drop you a line to say how nice it was to see you the other night. You were looking lovely as ever.
As I said, I'm working in London for a while. How about we meet up?
Take care, Squeaky.
Lots of love
Josh (the boss)

I'd tried so hard to get Josh out of my system over the last year and yet here I am with butterflies in my stomach, wondering what it means. I must have gone over every word of his email about ten times, and every time I scan his nickname for me, 'Squeaky', it's like my stomach does this stupid flip, and my eyes get all watery. And now I'm sitting here missing him. I keep telling myself to snap out of it, reminding myself that Josh totally betrayed me, but it doesn't work. Not now that they've split up. Josh and Megan splitting up, I'm ashamed to say, changes everything.

Carly came and stayed over tonight! I didn't mention the Josh email to her. I need to decide how I feel about it on my own first . . . and I'm pretty sure I know what her reaction will be.

Carly's finally plucked up the courage to go for an interview at Micky Samms in his flagship London salon. It would be so prestigous to work there – he's won British Hairdresser of the Year about five times.

It was so nice to see Carls. Although I felt a bit bad keeping the Josh thing secret from her; I usually tell her everything. And if anything ever does come of it then obviously I will. I'd asked Kassie if it would be OK if Carly stayed over. I was actually quite nervous after the *Hello!* thing, and worried she'd be pissed off with me, but she was fine. She was too busy ordering underwear off the Internet, while having her nails done by Sandra, her personal nail technician, to care.

'Oh that's nice, you have a lovely time. Get Ricardo to cook something nice for you, eh?' she said vaguely, examining her newly French-manicured left hand.

* * *

Carly was like a kid in a sweetshop when she arrived and I gave her a quick tour of the house. I didn't want to make it too obvious; it's not really my place to traipse people round the place after all and Mrs E's always on the prowl. But I couldn't help showing off, just a bit.

'OH MY GOD, Katie! This is AMAZING! It's incredible!' Carly gasped, when she saw my 'quarters'.

'I know, I know!' I squealed, 'God, it's fab that you're here, Carls. I've been dying for someone to actually see it. It's all very well describing it to everyone, but half the time I feel like they think I'm exaggerating. But as you can see . . . I'm actually not!'

Carly nodded, finally speechless, as I put on some music and poured a glass of wine for us both. We're usually Smirnoff Ice girls, but Ricardo had insisted on picking out a bottle of wine to go with the food he'd made. He was horrified that anyone would drink an alcopop with his wild-mushroom and rocket risotto with parmesan shavings!

'So, our Katie's got her picture in a magazine,' Carly said, smiling after I'd told her about the *Hello!* drama. 'You won't want to know us soon. Too busy hobnobbing with Elton and Cheryl Cole to bother with the ordinary folk.'

'You're right,' I sighed melodramatically. 'In fact,' I checked my watch, 'I can only spare you another hour tops, Carls. I'm expecting the WAGs over for some late night poker soon . . .'

'Shut up!' Carly threw a three-hundred-quid brocade cushion at my head. Then she swigged back the rest of her wine and glanced out of the window at the surveillance camera lurking outside. 'Bet you're being watched, though . . . 24/7! Now that's something I can relate to. Diane's been watching me like a hawk all week. Some bloody woman complained I'd botched her cut—'

Poor Carls. She put a good face on it but I could hear her voice wobble and she bit her bottom lip to keep it steady. Diane really gets to her.

'Don't let it get you down, Carls,' I soothed. I knew enough about Diane to know that she could turn any little thing into a reason to have a go at Carly, let alone a properly complaining client.

'Yeah, I know. She must have been in her fifties, this woman, and she came in with a picture of this, like, twenty-year-old with really thick hair, probably even extensions, and she's like, "I want to look like that." '

'Oh dear.' I shook my head.

'Exactly. I was like, "Your hair is very different to the model's," and I even got out more photosheets and mags to give her other ideas and she seemed to agree to compromise and I thought she was happy with what we'd decided, otherwise I never would have done it. And then she goes and complains to Diane. She was like, "It's not at all what we agreed. It's just not what I asked for." And, of course, it's all my fault and blah, blah, blah . . . Diane just let rip in front of the whole salon. Completely humiliated me. God, I hate that woman. And I'm really worried she'll give me a crappy reference for Micky Samms.'

'Well, don't get one from her,' I suggested. 'The other stylists know you're good, get one from one of them, or someone at the college. They're all on your side, aren't they?'

'Yeah, s'pose,' Carly agreed, not sounding too convinced. 'Anyway, I've got to get through the interview first,' she laughed. 'Here's me giving myself the job and I haven't set foot through the door yet.' She got a tissue out, blew her nose, and all of a sudden turned her frown upside down. Typical Carly. 'So,' she said. 'When does the mag come out? I could do with a laugh.'

'Tomorrow actually!' I grinned. 'I can't wait to see it. What time do you think your interview will finish?'

'Well, I've to be there at nine and then they've said to allow four hours because they're going to test my cutting and colouring, as well as having a chat with me. I feel sick just thinking about it.'

'You'll be fine,' I reassured her. 'Do you want a practice run . . . ?' I nodded towards the bag of tricks she'd brought with her. Scissors, combs, straighteners – all the tools of the trade.

'Nah, you're all right,' she sighed. 'If I don't know my stuff by now . . . well, it's a bit too late, isn't it?'

'Honestly, you'll be fantastic,' I said again. 'And I could come and meet you afterwards if you like. Maxi is at nursery and once I've sorted out the playroom and tidied a few of their bits away I'll be a free agent.'

'God, that would be great!' Carly grinned. 'I'm not

even sure I'll be able to find my way back to the station without you!'

'You wait till you live here,' I grinned. 'You'll be on and off that Tube like an old hand.'

'Can you imagine,' Carly said, 'you and me both in London, at the same time!'

Carly's interview went really well. It was a fairly junior position she'd gone for and they'd more or less offered her the job on the spot, with a view to moving up a step or two pretty swiftly, so she was absolutely made up when I met her for lunch afterwards.

'Let's have a drink to celebrate,' she said.

'Carls, I'd love to . . . but I can't, I'm still technically at work, remember? Got to get the kids at three.'

'Oh yeah. Well, I'm having one,' she grinned. 'Think I deserve it, don't you?'

'Absolutely,' I smiled. 'And look what I've got.'

'I reached into my bag and pulled out a copy of *Hello!* magazine.

'Are you in there?' Carly shrieked, snatching at the magazine.

I batted her hand away. 'Patience, Grasshopper.' I opened the magazine near the middle and flicked through a few pages until we got to the 'At Home with the Ballentines' spread.

And there I was, hovering discreetly behind the rest of the assembled family, in my completely ridiculous get-up. My first brush with the media. I scrutinized the picture. My hair was just wrong and my make-up more mannequin than usual. And as for the clothes – don't even go there. Carly summed it up with her usual forthrightness.

'I know it's you, Katie, and it sort of looks like you and everything, but it's so not you!'

Exclusive Interview with Kassie Ballentine
'I don't just swan around in Versace dresses all day!'
At Home with the Ballentines
Kassie Ballentine reveals what it's really like to be one half of football's most famous couple.

Kassie Ballentine is a real-life human dynamo. She's got more projects on the go than a class full of primary-school children and yet she still manages to juggle bringing up two children (Regan (5) and Maximus (3½), running two households in this country and one in Spain and being a loving wife to hubby Brett Ballentine. In this exclusive interview, Kassie explains how she does it, whether more kids are in the pipeline and just what else is in store for the future.

Being so much in the public eye, what impression do you think people have of you?

Oh, I'm sure lots of people think I'm a lazy so-and-so who swans about in designer dresses all day, but it's really not like that. I've got two growing children and although I have help with them and with running our homes, there's still a lot to organize. And that's before I've even started trying to get my own projects up and running.

Regan and Maxi are such lovely children, do you and Brett have any plans to have any more?

To be honest, no. Brett and I are both so such busy people. We don't think you should bring children into the world if you haven't got time to spend with them. Obviously bringing up our kids is the most important thing we'll ever do, but as both our careers pick up, I don't think it would be fair on the child to have another one. Obviously, if time were no object I'd have half a dozen – I just love children so much!

Speaking of children, you've just got a new nanny (Katie Meredith, 18). How's that working out?

Katie's really lovely with the kids. Of course, we were very careful about choosing someone to look after them – it's the most important job in the world.

Do you prefer being based in London or spending time at your home in Yorkshire?

Well, obviously we're more bound to London because Brett plays for a London club. But when he has a game up north or a bit of time off, we love to spend time up there. I adore the countryside – and of course the children's grandparents on their dad's side are up there. As my own parents aren't really around, my family now is the most important thing in my life.

Your home is exquisitely decorated. Did you get the designers in or do you prefer the personal touch?

We did get an interior designer in to help us, but he was very much guided by what we wanted. I couldn't live somewhere that didn't express the real me.

And what do you have planned for the future, Kassie?

Well, my lingerie range is continuing to do quite well; there are some new designs coming out in time for Christmas. And, of course, my exercise video which will also be out later this year.

You're looking fantastic. What's the secret? Do you have a diet and exercise regime?

Oh no, I think I'm quite lucky really, I'm just naturally slim. I would never starve myself or anything like that. I eat like a horse! Although I suppose I do eat pretty healthily on the whole, but every now and then the kids and I will tuck into a big plate of chips together – delicious!

Kassie, thanks very much for taking the time to see us in your beautiful home.

Hot News!
KASSIE'S CROWNING GLORY

Kassie Ballentine's no stranger to the bleach bottle, but it turns out her latest lightened locks are in fact . . . a wig! Kassie (24) has worked her way through almost every style and colour over the years, but this time she's avoided the snip. When Kassie stepped out in Rome with the sleek new bob, onlookers simply assumed she was catching up on the latest trend. The wig is a dramatic change from the long tousled tresses she's been sporting in recent months.

Reveal's verdict: Like the cut but a warmer tone would be better for Kassie's skin.

13

We're off to Yorkshire next week. Brett's got a midweek match in Manchester and then the rest of the week off. I'm going up with the kids and Ted on Wednesday and Kassie's following on at the weekend. Apparently she's got a very important meeting with a Botox needle that she doesn't want to miss. Kassie's very open about all her treatments. She hasn't had any major surgery yet (except her boob job, which she says she doesn't count as it was more of a career move than a cosmetic procedure!) but she's had just about everything else: Botox, chemical peels, veneers on her teeth. She even had a couple of collagen jabs to her lips before she got too freaked out by the possibility of ending up looking like a permanently pouting cod.

'I don't see that it's any different to wearing make-up, Katie,' she said to me last night. 'If there's stuff available to give Nature a little helping hand, why not make the most of it?'

She actually invited me to a Botox party, too. I don't know if she seriously expected me to take her up on it. I mean, hello! I'm eighteen! And call me old-fashioned, but I have a slight twitch over the thought of someone sticking a needle full of bacteria into my face.

'Mind you,' Kassie said, 'you're still quite young and firm, aren't you? Before I had kids my body was so fantastic . . . now it's ruined. And as for wrinkles – I tell you, it's all those sleepless nights. It's a wonder I don't look worse than I do.'

Hmm, whatever you say, Kassie . . .

To: joshsparkym@hotletters.com
From: kmeredith@eggspok.com
RE: Long time no email

Hi Josh
Yeah, meeting up would be cool. I'm off to Yorkshire for a week but will be back in London for the foreseeable after that. Let me know when you're going to be in town and we can arrange something.
Love
Katie

Watch this space.

The journey to Yorkshire was pretty uneventful. Ted and me and the two kids were chauffeured there so I didn't need to worry about driving. In fact the most stressful thing I'd had to do all morning was pack for the children. I mean, they've both got hundreds of items of clothing each and about a hundred pairs of shoes – I'm not joking. Every time Kassie goes shopping (which, let's face it, is a pretty regular occurrence) she comes back with a little (inappropriate) something for the kids. So I ended up filling two massive suitcases full of stuff just for them. My own bags looked meagre by comparison.

We had about half an hour of I Spy on the way, but fortunately they both got bored with that game pretty quickly and settled down to watch an in-car DVD instead. So the four hours to the country pile passed pretty quickly.

And what a pile it is. I've never been this far north (not too far from York itself) and the countryside is really beautiful. And the Ballentines' house – or, rather, mansion – is set in a really amazing bit of rolling countryside. It's kind of hidden away from the road by a woodland bit which then opens up where the house is resting on top of this hill with a stunning view down into a valley and then to the moors beyond.

Inside, the house is like a replica of a stately home, all olde worldy with lots of dark heavy furniture and dark heavy fabric. Not really my thing – I think I must have been brainwashed by the guys at IKEA. I just want light, airy and minimalist, thank you very much!

But when it comes to luxury, it's all up to Ballentine standard. Every possible need is catered for – huge bedrooms with stunning views and en suites, staff at your beck and call night and day, and more loos than the whole of our street in Hastings. Nan would be so proud. Outside, a sweeping gravel driveway veers off to a converted stable, where an Alfa Romeo Spider sports car, a Mercedes and a vintage Jaguar are all lovingly maintained by Stokes, the butler/valet/handyman/gardener all rolled into one. And last but not least, the kids' rooms each have an entire wardrobe of summer and winter clothes waiting for them. So much for angst about packing. Thanks for telling me, Mrs E!

Kassie wasn't due to join us until Saturday, which meant a reprieve from her twenty-a-day habit, thank God. And Brett was playing an evening match. So I got the kids all fed and watered and ready for bed and promised them that Daddy would come and give them a kiss when he got home, which wouldn't be until late, as he was playing in Manchester. I decided to leave him a note. It took me about an hour to compose it. I wasn't quite sure of the note etiquette between us; mainly, how I should address him. Ridiculous, but true. It then took me another half hour to decide where to leave it (one of the hall tables) as the place was so big it wasn't like you'd just stumble over it.

Brett
Arrived safely with kids. All tucked up in bed. Promised you'd look in on them on your return. Hope that's OK.
Katie

I absolutely fell into bed at the end of the day. All this getting used to luxury stately homes is so exhausting, darling.

The next morning I'd got the children up and dressed and they were in the middle of their breakfast in the kitchen when their dad put in an appearance.

'Daddy!' they shrieked, leaping off their chairs and nearly bowling him over as he crouched down to hug them.

Brett is a different person up in Yorkshire, it seems. Just like, well, just like an ordinary dad. Kassie would be snapping about dirty hands on designer fabric by now but Brett was quite happy to let them clamber all over him. 'Guess who's coming to stay for the weekend?' he asked, knowing full well the kids already knew the answer.

'Granny and Grandad!' they squealed.

'Yeah!' Brett laughed, straightening up and tousling their hair. 'So eat up all your breakfast and you'll have plenty of energy for when Granny and Grandad get here.'

He guided them back to the table. 'Morning, Katie,' he said, without making eye contact with me. 'Thanks for the note.'

Granny and Grandad Ballentine – Brett's parents – are great. Grandad appeared a real gruff Yorkshireman at first, but underneath he's just a really sweet old fella with a twinkle in his eye. And Granny is homely and a bit bossy – just like a granny should be. They must have had Brett quite late in life because they are definitely loads older than my parents and they quite obviously dote on him and their grandchildren. Seeing Brett with them was quite an eye-opener, too. He was really respectful – he even seemed a bit in awe of his dad. And his mum had him doing the dishes within a couple of hours!

The kids were in absolute seventh heaven. Undivided attention from Daddy and grandparents – what bliss!

In a way I felt like a bit of a spare part, and if I'm honest I was just a tiny bit put out at how quickly the kids switched allegiance from me to their beloved grandparents. I know, it's pathetic. It's how it should be, of course. Maybe it was me feeling a bit unloved. Miles from home and family and . . . No, I am determined not to think about Josh. I know all the cuddles in the world don't make up for what he did. And if he's done it once, he'll do it again, as my mum said when it all kicked off.

'Better off out of it,' she'd told me. 'You deserve better, Katie.' Well, maybe I do, but sitting there on the velvet chaise longue, watching Maxi and Regan snuggling up to Brett's mum and dad, it didn't feel that way.

But there was Saturday to look forward to – the day earmarked as my pampering day, courtesy of Kassie. A whole day of TLC, just for me!

Saturday, early evening, and I have just enjoyed a glorious day of healthy self-indulgence. Japanese facial booster and full body massage to name just two of the divine treatments on offer. I feel like a different person; as though I am floating along like one of those characters out of *Gosford Park*. Out of my bedroom window, I have a view to die for. The sun is setting, there is nothing but fields and hedges for miles and miles, and I am wrapped up in my delicate Chinese silk dressing gown (yes, a present from you-know-who way back when), checking my emails on my new BlackBerry (flash, huh? It was a present from Mum and Dad for my eighteenth!). Anyway, amongst the spam and junk mail, I picked up an email from the rat himself, Josh Markham. I tried so very hard not to feel smug about that, but come on, I am human – give me a break! He wants to set up a date for our drink in London, apparently. Hmm. A bit too keen if you ask me – or is he trying to build bridges? Oh why did I reply in the first place? I decided to leave it a bit before I got back to him. The more I think about it, the less sure I am about meeting him alone . . . I better not do anything hasty. I'll sleep on it first.

A day after my pampering extravaganza, and that floaty feeling has vanished. Kassie arrived on Saturday night and has already stirred up a hornet's nest of trouble with the in-laws. I put the children in bed, and decided to go and thank her for my day. I could hear voices in the living room and headed there, but when I walked in, the atmosphere . . . well, you could have cut it with a knife. Kassie was perched on one end of the sofa, cigarette already lit, with the mardiest expression on her face. Brett's mum and dad were looking pretty tight-lipped, too, and Brett, he just looked downright uncomfortable.

'There you are,' Kassie barked rudely as I came in. She turned to her parents-in-law. 'Seeing as you are intent on keeping my children from me tomorrow, I'm sure *Katie* won't mind coming shopping with me,' she told them. 'I mean, I thought it might be nice for my children to spend time with me, but clearly you've all been plotting and scheming behind my back . . . as usual.' Snatching up her ashtray, and stalked past me out of the door. 'Be ready for ten-thirty tomorrow morning, Katie,' she threw over her shoulder. 'We're driving into Leeds with Dave. It's not like you'll be needed around here. Granny and Grandpa have got it all sorted.' You could virtually feel the sarcasm oozing out of her on to the floor. And with that she stomped upstairs, leaving me loitering like a dummy with Brett and his parents.

I was pretty annoyed. Kassie's little spat wasn't anything to do with me and I didn't see why she should begrudge the gramps seeing their grandchildren for the day. I mean, it wasn't as if they got the opportunity very often. And anyway, shopping! Did Kassie seriously think two kids under five would enjoy traipsing round a mall, while she picked out fancy underwear? And why the urgent need to do it now, when she could do it anytime in London? It was petty jealousy, that was what it was.

I looked awkwardly at Brett, trying to convey to him that I wasn't in any way taking sides. But fortunately he came to my rescue. 'Don't worry, Katie, you go shopping tomorrow with Kassie, it'll be fine.'

I exhaled the breath I hadn't even realized I'd been holding. 'Er . . . oh . . . um . . . OK,' I said lamely and turned to leave the room.

'By the way,' he asked my back, 'did you have at nice day at the spa?'

Nice of him to remember, I suppose. 'Yes, I came down to thank you,' I said, hardly bothering to turn around. 'I'm quite . . . er . . . tired, er, yeah, um, I'll just head off to bed.' I managed a weak smile. 'Night then,' I said, waving limply towards Granny and Grandad.

'Goodnight, dear,' they said, kindly. But before I was even out of the room I could hear the subject was turning back to Kassie.

'Honestly Brett . . .' I heard as I walked towards the back stairs. But I wasn't going to stick around for the post mortem. It was depressing. Why can't people just be nice?

Just as I was settling myself into bed with a big mug of cocoa and a fat pile of Kassie's celebrity mags, my mobile rang. It was on my bedside table, and I nearly spilt half a mug of hot chocolate over my pyjamas, the ring seemed so loud and unexpected. I grabbed the phone and looked at the screen. Josh's name came up. No, I never did delete it – sad, I know, but sometimes I couldn't help looking at it and hoping he'd call and now he was. I felt the butterflies start while I decided whether or not to answer it. But in the end . . .

'Hello?' I tried to sound quizzical crossed with nonchalant.

'Hi, Katie . . . It's Josh.'

'Oh, hi, Josh.' Casual, distracted this time.

'Sorry it's a bit late. I got your email.'

'Email? Oh, right . . . that email. Sorry I'm a bit vague.

I've been a bit rushed off my feet. We're up in Yorkshire . . . it's all go.' God, I could feel my nose growing by the second. 'You wanted to meet up?'

'Well, yes, if you can find the time,' Josh started to tease. 'Fit it into your hectic schedule . . .'

I nearly giggled.

'Should be able to fit it in at some point,' I said, feigning a humour bypass 'When were you thinking?' I pretended to be leafing through a diary – which was actually one of Regan's colouring books I'd accidentally bought upstairs along with the magazines.

'Well, I'm free most nights. Tell you what – you have a think about when you might be free and email me. I'll fit round you. I'm going to be working in Waterloo, but I could come over your way? It's up to you.'

He was being way too nice and considerate. I could see this hard act of mine wasn't going to last long. 'Right, well Waterloo's fine,' I said, in a much more friendly manner. 'I'll talk to Livvy, the night nanny for the kids, she's a real London girl and see if she knows any good bars, and I'll email you back about the date, OK?' I felt a bit nervous now. I couldn't quite believe I was arranging to meet the Hound of the Baskervilles.

But it was as if Josh could read my mind. 'Katie, I . . .' He sounded suddenly serious. 'I think I should tell you how sorry I am.'

Oh, no. Before I could stop them, tears were welling up. I couldn't speak.

'Last year and everything . . .' He cleared his throat. 'I was an idiot, I'm sorry, the way I treated you . . . it was . . . well . . . it was wrong . . .' He paused again. 'You didn't deserve it.' He said the last bit really softly and it was taking everything I had not to succumb to the melting feeling inside me.

'It's OK,' I sighed. 'It's in the past, what's done is done.' Nice line in clichés, Katie. 'I mean, yes, you were out of order and no, I didn't deserve it but, well, I've had time to get over it and y'know, maybe we can be friends again. Well, see if . . . that would . . .'

'That would be really perfect,' Josh finished for me. 'You're one in a million,' he said. 'You know that?'

And once again I couldn't answer. But this time it was because I couldn't get my lips to uncurl the smile that was creeping across my face.

Hotline magazine

Bouncing Baby Ballentine on the Way

Brett and Kassie Ballentine are overjoyed to be expecting their second baby in May 2004. The couple, who already have a daughter, Regan (1), can't wait to greet the new arrival. 'We were so excited – I took the test about five times just to be sure!' Bless – it can be tricky seeing that really obvious blue line, Kassie!

14

Actually, hitting the town with Kassie was kind of fun, if a little bizarre. She is certainly a demon shopper. If she even slightly likes something, she buys it. And she's supposed to be all inconspicuous, so she's wearing the WAG staples of baseball cap and a massive pair of Nicole Ritchie shades in the middle of Leeds' Harvey Nicks. And then there's Dave, the big, burly, unmistakable bodyguard who lurches along behind us . . . Way to go unnoticed, Kassie!

There was even a 'pap' on the prowl. I have to hand it to them: they certainly do their homework. They just seem to know where to pop up and take the shot – or maybe they just make a point of hanging around in busy department stores on the off chance that a random celebrity might wander past with her entourage. And random, when it really comes down to it, is the operative word when it comes to Kassie's celebrity status.

'Oi! Kassie, Kassie sweetheart – give us a smile! Over here, Kassie.'

'Shit,' muttered Kassie and grabbed my arm. 'Keep your head down, Katie – don't want to encourage them,' she hissed, before holding her own head high and flashing a dazzling smile.

'Yeah, that's right. Lovely!'

Kassie shoved me forward in the general direction of our car, which was waiting for us down a side street outside the centre.

Dave, who likes to be referred to as 'security' and looks like he's just got out of a ten-year stretch in Broadmoor, gave his best menacing glare to the assembled onlookers. I reckon even the most tenacious of paparazzi might baulk at Dave, to be honest; he's a big guy.

'Whew,' said Kassie, settling into the leather-upholstered back seat of Dave's SUV. 'Bloody paps. Make my life a nightmare, don't they, Dave?'

As if, I thought with a grin. Like she wasn't loving every minute of the attention. She didn't fool me.

Still, we'd managed to pack in quite a bit of shopping. Or rather, Kassie had managed it. Wedged between us was an array of designer goodies: an Armani jacket, Gina shoes, a three-grand Gucci dress – not to mention a new quilted Chanel clutchbag-purse thing, which she'd probably only use once. Sticks in my craw (Nan's expression, isn't it great!), spending all that money on designer gear. It's just a bit sick. Or maybe I've got a lot to learn. After all, if you've got it, flaunt it. That's what they say, isn't it?

But what was more glaringly obvious than ever when we'd been trailing through the shops and out again, is that Kassie just doesn't eat!

We'd been on the go since nine with only a bottle of mineral water each to sustain us and I was absolutely starving – my stomach was literally growling. But when I tried to make noises about getting some food she just kind of body-swerved the issue and dived into the next designer-frock shop. In the end I made an excuse about wanting to go and buy my sister a present and went off for half an hour in search of a Big Mac. And I swear when I got back I could see her nose twitching. She must have been starving. It's no wonder that woman's so skinny. She survives on thin air. At least she agreed to stop and have a coffee – or a cup of hot water with a slice of lemon in it for Kassie. And we almost had a civilized conversation for once.

'What do you think of Brett's parents?' she asked me in a mock-casual kind of way.

Oh, no, I so did not want to go here. 'Yeah, fine, I mean I haven't really spent much time with them, but they seem OK.' Is that vague enough for you?

'Yeah, they are,' Kassie sighed. 'They bloody hate me, though.'

My mouth opened and closed several times, 'Well, I . . .'

'Oh, don't look so scared, sweetheart, I know they do. They blame me for taking their precious little boy away from them. Honestly, you'd think Brett was still twelve the way they treat him. And he had this girlfriend, Beth, when he was really young who they just *loved*. Thought the sun shone out of her you-know-where.' She smiled at me, but there was something not very nice behind the smile. 'Girl-next-door type, you know, butter wouldn't melt. Not like me, eh?' She nudged me with her elbow.

I smiled lamely. Far be it from me to agree with her.

'And then I came along and as far as they're concerned I'm like the wicked witch. Doesn't matter that I do loads of stuff for charity and lugged around two bloody enormous grandchildren for them for nine months – and that's before you even think about being sliced open to get the bloody things out. Oh no, that counts for nothing. Just because of my past and the fact that I don't have a problem speaking my mind you'd think I kebabbed babies for a hobby or something . . .'

I winced.

'Not that I care. What can they do about it? Brett would never leave me. He's much too weak.'

I stared ahead of me, not sure where we were going with this, and then, just like that, Kassie's back to bright and breezy mode. She's rummaging through one her bags, taking out a sequinned vest.

'Ooh, Katie. This is sooo your colour. Why don't you have it? My treat.'

It was like she was trying to buy me on side. I felt really sorry for her then. She couldn't help being who she was . . . could she?

A BOY FOR BRETT

Proud parents Brett and Kassie Ballentine couldn't wait to
show off the newest addition to their family. The London
Spartacus FC striker (25) and Kassie (25) happily posed for
photographs with newborn son, Maximus, outside the
exclusive Portland Hospital in London as they prepared to
take him home.

Brett, looking uncharacteristically cheerful, said, 'I'm over
the moon. I'm absolutely made up – I can't believe I'm the
father of two.'

Son Maximus weighed 7lb 3oz and was delivered by
planned Caesarian section last Wednesday.

'I think Maximus looks more like his mum than me,' a
delighted Brett said. But let's see whether it's your talent for
football or her talent for spending money he's inherited!

15

Back in London, things were back to normal – or as normal as anything ever is round here. Carly came up to go flat-hunting, and after traipsing round half of the city, she finally found somewhere. A huge flat in Islington, sharing with two nurses. Carly's thrilled – Islington is great for nightlife, and for shopping. I was a teeny bit envious, I have to admit. Especially since Carly seemed to bond so quickly with her prospective flatmates. I felt just a little bit excluded, and kind of trapped, living where I was in the Ballentine open prison. Yeah, it's a dream come true, but I can hardly let my hair down with the kids. Watching Carly laughing and making plans, I suddenly realized I was missing out on a lot of fun. I'm a teenager, for God's sake. Where did my life go?

'So how was Yorkshire?' Carly asked me as we sat on the bus back to the Ballentines'. 'How was the spa?'

'Amazing,' I said dreamily. 'I could have stayed there for ever. I can see why the rich folk get so addicted to all those treatments. But cheap it ain't. I clocked some of the prices and I'm telling you, that day cost Kassie practically a month's worth of my salary! Guess she isn't me-me-me all the time. I felt brilliant at the end of it – and all the stuff just smells good enough to eat.'

'And what's their place like?' Carly wanted to know. 'Standard stately home in rolling countryside, correct?'

'Correct,' I laughed. 'There's loads of staff and LOADS of rooms and it's all a bit much really. I mean, I bet Kassie hasn't even seen some bits of the house.'

'I take it you were staying in the West Wing, darling?' Carly said in her snootiest voice.

'Naturally, darling.' I paused. 'But there was a bit of a spat on Saturday night . . . Between Kassie and the in-laws . . .'

Carly leaned in closer. 'Oh, yeah? Do tell.'

I lowered my voice, just in case there was a spy on the bus (you never know). 'Well, Lady K reckons it's because of her past and everything. And before K came along, Mr B had some old flame, Beth, who the old folks really rated. K's got a chip on her shoulder about it all. She reckons B's parents don't think she's good enough for their precious boy.'

'Well, I suppose you can see their point of view. I mean, is it the kind of career you'd be proud to tell your kids about?' Carly said sanctimoniously.

'Well, Lady K doesn't seem too bothered. As far as she's concerned it was a way to earn an honest living. If some bloke was happy enough to hand over his cash to see her gyrating for half an hour, why shouldn't she have done it? It's not like she mugged anyone.'

'Yeah, but it's a bit on the degrading side, isn't it? I mean, I think I'd clean toilets first.'

'Yeah well,' I joked, 'with your body you might have to!'

'Oi!' Carly swung out at me as I ducked out of her way. It was good to have a friend in town – and at that point I didn't even realize how much I was going to need her.

Revelations (2004)

KASSIE FIGHTS THE FLAB

Kassie Ballentine's on track to shed nearly two stone to get back to her pre-pregnancy super-shape.

She'll do it by eating small portions of grilled meats and raw vegetables. She's ditched crisps for sweet potato fries, knocking off 610 calories a portion.

And out go the regular 430-calorie frappuccinos, and in come the 290-calorie smoothies.

'Even before she gave birth Kassie began working with a nutritionist, a trainer and her vocal coach to get her back in shape,' says an insider.

She will have to wait six weeks after her Caesarean to hit the new treadmill she's had installed in the gym at her London home.

But health experts say she can hit the ground running – by breastfeeding baby Maximus, which will really burn up those calories.

16

Oh God. Don't tell me I'm falling for JM all over again? Maybe I wasn't really as over him as I thought.

I met him on Wednesday under the clock at Waterloo station. Livvy had told me about this gastropub on The Cut where you can get nice food so I was planning to take him there. I made sure I didn't arrive early – I didn't want to look like I was keen or anything. Plus I knew I'd just get nervous if I was hanging around waiting, convinced he might stand me up.

But as it was, he was right there, standing in front of me when I stepped off the escalator.

I wish it had been awkward, that we'd had nothing to say to each other, that I didn't take one look at him and melt. I'd like to say it was all an anticlimax. It would be so much simpler. But it was too easy. It was like we had never split up. 'Two peas in a pod', my nan used to say about us when we were together. Damn.

We moved towards a booth in the corner of the pub. I hadn't noticed in the club, but Josh had grown his hair a bit longer. It looked all chestnutty and tousled and I had to resist the urge to reach out and stroke it. His eyes were all sparkly and hazelnut-coloured. My knees were getting weak before we'd even sat down.

Josh seemed a bit quiet at first. Kept fiddling with the wine list, opening and shutting it. Then he gave me this look – the same look he'd given me when he'd told me about him and Megan. Serious, contrite, that kind of look. Here we go, I thought, feeling the panic rising. Another Josh bombshell I so didn't need. What was I doing here?

Then he cleared his throat.

'You know on the phone the other night? What I said about being sorry?'

My beating heart slowed a little in relief. I started to shush him.

'No, Katie, let me finish. 'Cos . . . well, 'cos I meant it. I was an idiot. Megan was . . .'

I felt my cheeks redden. I couldn't even bear to hear him say her name.

'Well, she's not who I thought she was, Katie,' he said. 'She's a bit a of cow, really. Who knew?'

I did, for a start! I nearly opened my mouth to deliver a snide 'I told you so' response. I'd be lying if I said there wasn't some pleasure in hearing him stick the knife into her.

'It took you long enough to find that out,' I snapped.

He sighed. 'It was a bit of weird one, Katie, honestly. She's like, really insecure and every time I'd say I was through with her she'd start threatening to do things . . .'

I looked confused.

'You know, like hurt herself and stuff.' Josh looked so forlorn all of a sudden. 'I mean at first I fell for it but after a while the penny dropped . . . you know, like this was going to go on for ever, and I couldn't really take responsibility for it . . .' He fixed me with his perfect gaze. 'I'm so sorry, Katie.' His voice came out in almost a whisper. I reached across and smoothed his hair away from his eyes. He put his hand to mine and our fingers intertwined. He drew me towards him. I resisted for about ten seconds before I was kissing him. Those lovely, soft lips had lost none of their magic . . . I was falling all over again.

I went back to the hotel he'd been put up in. And even though we slept in the same bed, nothing happened. Well, *that* didn't happen. Josh held me. I had so missed those muscular arms around me. It felt right to be there in his bed, his chest gently rising and falling with every breath, his tousled hair mingling with mine.

Carly's going to have a fit when she finds out. My mum and dad won't be too chuffed either, not after they had to deal with the fallout from our break-up last time. I stroked Josh's ear softly with my fingertip and snuggled in closer to his neck. No one need know for now, I thought. This is just between me and Josh.

It's gone a bit quiet at Ballentine Towers. Kassie's video's about to be launched and she's never at home. She's dashing round the country on a promotional tour (organized by Creepy Ken, of course). He's managed to get her on every

chat show, on every channel, and on ⌐
She's even had a couple of staged even⌐
centres, or 'focus group malls' as she likes⌐
about the cat who got the cream. And sh⌐
seriously. I mean, for example, she was o⌐
Show the other day and she was going on and on about how
if you do something the wrong way it just looks tacky,
whereas if it's done the right way it's really classy. And he's
like virtually rolling his eyes at her and sniggering because
her exercise video is like something off *Little Britain*. She's in
this too-tight hot-pink leotard with sweat bands and a high
pony-tail and a whole tanker-load of foundation and make-
up, rounded off with a pair of sparkly leg-warmers. And
she's got this perma-tanned uber-camp fitness instructor
(Tony – or 'super-toned Tony' as he likes to call himself . . .
I'm not joking!) helping her out in a pair of what look like
overstuffed Speedos (ew!). And I was one of the first people
to get a sneak preview. Yes, Kassie ordered me to have a
'girls' night in' with her so that she could show off the video.
I didn't know where to put myself – I've never been a very
good liar. But fortunately, Kassie mistook my frozen,
horrified expression as rapt admiration. I feel a bit sorry for
her really. She hasn't got a clue.

Brett's still in the thick of it with training and matches,
half of which are away games, so it's pretty much down to
me (and Ted from time to time) to do the parenting. There's
even a cover nanny at the moment for my weekends off.
Poor little Regan and Maximus, they hardly see Mummy

.ddy these days. Mrs E says that as soon as the football
,on's finished and Brett has a bit of time off, it's a
different story, and you never see the kids because they
spend all their time with their dad. I hope that's true – for
their sakes.

Ted and I have been trying to make the most of it for
them. Today we went to the park and the boating lake with
the kids. The weather was beautiful, really bright, crisp and
autumnal, and I felt good. I was still buzzing a little from
seeing Josh. I deliberately fought back the urge to set a date
for our wedding and decided to play it cool. I'm not falling
into that love trap again, not this time, or not yet, anyway.
Josh seems to be respecting my feelings, too. He hasn't
pushed it. There have been phone calls, but I am taking
things very slowly.

I haven't said anything to Carly either. I just can't face
seeing her expression when I tell her. I knew I shouldn't
really have gone back with him so soon. I thought I'd got my
life back on track and was starting to feel sane again. As my
mum would say, sometimes I haven't got the sense I was
born with.

Heat (2005)

'I didn't starve myself thin.'

Kassie Ballentine shares the secret to how she lost her baby
weight . . . and just what do her and Brett get up to in the
bedroom?

**You lost all your baby weight really quickly. Did
you starve yourself?**
No! I wanted to do a fitness video (which I'm just in the
planning stages of now) and there was no way I'd even
contemplate doing my routines in front of a camera without
getting in shape first. You have to remember I've always
been a dancer, so I've always been pretty fit. But yes, I was
focused and I did start watching what I ate about two weeks
after I'd had Maximus.

Wow! That must have been hard.
Yeah, it was. But Brett's a very hands-on dad so he looked
after Maximus and we had other help.

So you didn't breastfeed.
No. I think it's a bit antisocial so I didn't bother. Anyway, I
don't want my boobs dropping round my ankles, do I!

I don't suppose Brett does either.
(Laughs) Now that would be telling. Besides at the moment I
think we're both too knackered to even think about getting
jiggy!

18

I am in big trouble.

I came back after dropping Regan and Maxi off (it's Wednesday, so it's nursery day), walked into the kitchen to clear up their breakfast stuff and there's Kassie holding a newspaper and glaring at me like I'm something really unpleasant she's just put her Manolos in.

I didn't have a clue what was going on, though I had a feeling it had something to do with me and what was in the paper – but then I drew a blank. I didn't talk to any reporters. I never would.

'Morning, Kassie,' I venture, my voice coming out almost a whisper, I'm so nervous. 'Is everything OK?'

Apparently everything was very much not OK.

'How dare you, you little bitch!' Kassie was practically white with anger. It was terrifying, I don't mind telling you. I had no idea what she was talking about. She sort of thrust the paper towards me. 'Look at it,' she snarled. 'Your f***ing chavvy relatives calling me an unfit mother!'

I stared at the page, still reeling, unable to take anything in. I could see the picture of me and Ted and the other picture of Kassie but panic had taken over and my brain was having trouble computing.

Ted and I had obviously been papped when we took the kids to the park. I mean, that's OK, the children's faces have been blurred and it's not like we're not allowed to take them out anywhere—

'Here,' she screamed, jabbing at the paper, 'let me help you out.' She put her face right up close to mine. 'Talk about me a lot, do you?' Her voice had gone a bit sing-song. I really thought she might swing for me, or grab my hair or scratch me or something, she looked so wild.

Oh no, how could this be happening to me? 'A source close to the nanny, Katie Meredith (18), told the *Sun* exclusively that this happens all the time and that although Dad is busy playing football Mum is busy . . . you guessed it . . . shopping!' I could just die.

I did a panicked rewind in my head of what conversations I had had with whom over the past few weeks. And who would be most likely to have blabbed to the press. Discounting Carly and Josh, obviously, I arrived at the inevitable conclusion: Auntie Chelle. Can't keep her trap shut for one minute, that woman. Family loyalty means nothing to her, never has. She'd gone to the tabloids hoping to make some fast cash out of what she must have thought was low-level libel. Insulting, but not shocking. Stupid woman. Wait till I got my hands on her! Some sleazebag from the *Sun* had then waited for an incriminating photo op – me and Ted large as life in the park (Maxi bouncing along on Ted's shoulders and Regan swinging along hand-in-hand with me) and an accompanying picture of Kassie browsing in Knightsbridge. Kassie was spitting feathers.

I wanted to say something to defend myself but I felt completely paralysed. I even still had one hand on the paper. Kassie grabbed my arm in a disturbingly firm grip.

'You stupid little cow,' she spat. 'It's nothing to you, is it? You think you can just swan off home and start mouthing off—'

'It's not like that . . .' I stammered, trying to defend myself. 'It's—'

'What exactly is it like, then?' she shouted before her voice went all wheedling. '"Kassie's such a lazy cow . . . I do all the work . . . those poor children . . ."' she mimicked shrilly. 'You selfish little bitch. You have no idea—'

'Kassie? What the hell is going on?' Brett's solid form blocked the doorway.

Oh God, I thought, here we go. It's all going to hit the fan now. I mean, let's face it, Brett's never really liked me at the best of times and now . . . well, to say I've really stuffed things up would be an understatement. I mean, I've signed a confidentiality clause . . . I could get fired! My heart lurched. Maxi and Regan, oh no, I couldn't bear it. I'd so totally let them down.

I stared at my feet. Go on, Brett Ballentine, do your worst, I thought miserably. I couldn't feel any more stupid anyway.

'Oh give it a rest, Kass,' Brett said. Then more firmly, 'Let go of her.'

Kassie continued to stare icily at me for half a minute before she dropped my hand in disgust. 'You have not heard the end of this,' she snarled.

I kept my head bowed as she snatched the paper out of my hand.

'Little bloody blabbermouth,' Kassie snarled again, handing the paper to Brett and jabbing her finger at the offending line.

Brett sighed. Pity and disappointment, I thought. That would be even worse than anger.

'For goodness' sake, Kassie,' he said. 'Is that all? Is that all this is all about?' He laughed. He actually laughed. 'God, you're a nutcase sometimes!'

I still couldn't quite bring myself to lift my head, but I raised my eyes enough to sneak a peek at Brett's face. 'It's nothing,' he said again. 'It'll be chip paper tomorrow and no one will even care.'

'It's not the point,' Kassie said, still sounding angry. 'She . . .' She pointed fiercely in my direction. 'Can't be trusted.'

'What, because she told some relative that her and Ted took the kids out while you went shopping. Come on Kassie, it's hardly classified information, is it? Like some journo couldn't have worked that out for themselves. It's not the crime of the century. No one's saying you're shooting up heroin in the playroom, are they?'

Kassie looked slightly calmer. And I mean slightly.

'Yeah, well, it's all right for you. *You* can't be looking after the kids, you've got an important match to play but *me*, oh *I'm* such a trollop because I could be looking after my kids and yet I choose to go shopping!'

There was a bit of a deafening silence as Kassie's ridiculous statement hung in the air. Brett looked very close to stating the obvious, but wisely he just walked over to the kettle and switched it on.

I found myself sneaking a look up towards the door, just in time to see Mrs E pass by with a sly smile on her face. She must be loving this. I stared back down at the floor. I'd never really noticed it before – the tiles looked like real slate.

Brett calmly put a teabag in a mug. 'You're over-reacting, Kassie. Just drop it – have some dignity. It's the press, isn't it. That's what they do. You can't have them on side all the time.'

Kassie made a humphing noise. 'Yeah, but *she's* paid to be discreet, Brett.'

'Look, have you even asked Katie if she's said anything? Or have you been too busy jumping to conclusions? For God's sake, woman, when are you going to absorb the fact that the press twist things to get a story? You've had enough crap printed about you to know that by now. Katie could have said nothing for all we know – or she could have made an innocent remark, and someone decided to turn it into a story. Give the girl a break!'

Kassie sighed but shot me another glare. 'Don't think I'm forgetting about this, Katie,' she spat out.

'I'm really sorry, Kassie—' I started, but she was already heading out of the room.

'Save it!' she snapped back at me over her shoulder.

I felt a wave of nausea wash over me and leant on the table for support.

'I'm really sorry,' I said again to Brett and started snivelling. 'Honestly, I don't spread gossip to anybody. I'm really careful, but I might have said something really small . . .'

But Brett didn't seem bothered at all. He took a drink of tea, and then finally looked over at me. 'Katie, don't worry about it – it's something and nothing. Harmless, OK?' Was I imagining it or was he actually giving me a sort of half-smile?

I smiled back weakly. Harmless? Well, maybe the article was, but Kassie? She hadn't seemed very harmless just now. She'd seemed pretty vindictive, with her beautifully manicured nails digging into my arm.

Brett finished his tea and looked at his watch. He picked up the car keys from the table. 'I'm going out,' he said. 'Tell her not to wait up, will you?'

The Sun (2007)

The Ballentine Babies Have a Fun Day Out with the Nanny and the Minder Whilst Mum Goes Shopping!

Little Regan and Maximus Ballentine seem to be having a whale of a time as they spend the day with their new nanny in Regent's Park. There are ducks to feed and squirrels to chase – what more could the five- and three-year-olds want? Well, perhaps to spend that precious time with their mum? But of course, we all know Kassie Ballentine (28) has much more important things to do . . . like shopping! A source close to the nanny, Katie Meredith (18), told the *Sun* exclusively that this happens all the time and that although Dad is busy playing football Mum is busy . . . you guessed it . . . shopping! 'Katie gets quite upset,' our source said. 'She loves the children and can't understand why their mum doesn't want to spend more time with them.' Nor can we, but then again, when there are Gucci bags to buy . . . Come on, Kassie – get your priorities right. They won't be little for ever, you know!

19

A few days later and Kassie's still not speaking to me.

Frankly, it's getting a bit boring now. I mean, at first I was full of guilt. Mortified at Auntie Chelle's 'indiscretion'. But now, well, let's put this into perspective, shall we?

When I think of the stuff I could be selling to the tabloids. Like that fact that since I've been here I don't think a day has gone by where I haven't heard Brett and Kassie arguing with each other. Half the time it's nothing major, but their rows are so bitchy. Nasty. My mum and dad never speak to each other like that. At first I thought it was all down to Brett; he's always being so sarky towards her. But now, having witnessed her Woman on the Edge of a Nervous Breakdown act on more than one occasion – I'm beginning to see things from Brett's position.

Mrs E keeps giving me these funny looks, too. I like to think they are sympathetic, looks, but I don't really trust her.

'Honestly, that Kassie's a right cow,' Carly said to me when I told her what had happened. 'You haven't even done anything, Katie – not knowingly anyway. But I'm sure she'll come round. After all, what would she do without you?'

Well, get another nanny, probably. But bless Carly for trying.

I'd finally plucked up the courage to tell Carly about spending the night with Josh. I figured it was quite a good week to break the news, as it might just get buried under the whole Kassie nightmare. Carly couldn't be too harsh with me, not when I was so hard done by . . . And the thing is, when it came to it, Carly was pretty unfazed by my devastating revelation.

'I knew that was coming,' she said. 'Can't honestly say I'm surprised. But that doesn't mean I trust the boy any further than I could throw him. Still, it's your life, your feelings, your business – I can't tell you what to do. Just be careful, OK?'

God, that was a load off. 'Thanks, Carls.' I smiled. 'It's not going to be like before, you know. I'm treading very carefully this time. For now, Josh and I are just good friends.' That was kind of true, too. Josh and I have spoken on the phone a lot since our 'date', but we haven't seen each other, and I haven't suggested it. He has been really supportive over 'Kassiegate'.

'Don't start feeling guilty, Katie,' he'd said when I told him. 'The Ballentines thrive on stuff like this – tabloid gossip. I mean, what else has Kassie got about her that's newsworthy? She's not exactly the talented half of that relationship, is she? She loves the attention, good or bad. She's being a hypocrite.'

Put like that, it made me feel a whole lot better. Josh was right – Kassie's behaviour was hypocritical, and she's made me feel like a criminal! She can't have her cake and eat it too. It's not fair.

Hotline magazine (2005)

Awww! Look at the baby Ballentines

Nice to see the little Ballentines still looking impossibly cute
– and too young to complain about the matching outfits!
And with Daddy there to lend a helping hand it looks like the
Ballentine babes are having a bounce-tastic time.

20

At last, a reprieve from the dog house. Kassie's all sweetness and light again. She's been a total cow for weeks and now, hey presto! She's nice as pie.

'Oh, Katie, which belt goes best with these jeans? What do you think?'

'Oh, Katie, Sandra's coming over to do my nails later. Do you want yours doing?'

And then, 'Oh, Katie, did I mention, Saturday, Brett's playing at home and we're all going to watch the match? That'll be fun, won't it!'

Oh, I get it. Off we all go to the match and sit together, Mummy and Nanny the best of friends, watching Daddy playing football, what a lucky pair the little Ballentines are.

Josh and I have now seen each other a few times since 'that night'. We've been to the cinema, and a couple of exhibitions. We even went out for a posh dinner in the West End. Josh saved all his pennies and took me to Nobu – a totally cool posh sushi restaurant in Mayfair! Bless him, he hates sushi, but he knows I love it. At one point I thought he was going to start gnawing at the damask tablecloth he was so hungry. He had to dash into McDonald's on the way home and buy about three Big Macs, which kind of took the glamour off the end of the evening. But I was on cloud nine that night, and not even the smell of reconstituted cardboard fries could bring me down. And my favourite bit was when we came back to my place and snuggled up together on the sofa.

Like everybody else, Josh is pretty impressed with the Ballentines' joint.

'I can't believe how much stuff they've got, Katie,' he said to me. 'They can't even be aware of half of it. I mean, if stuff went missing I don't suppose they'd even notice.'

'S'pose not,' I said, rooting through the box of chocs Josh had bought for me to find the one with the caramel centre. I located the one I was after and tucked myself back under Josh's arm, my head resting on his chest.

'You should flog something online,' he said.

'Yeah, right!' I snorted. 'Firstly, online auctions aren't quite my thing and secondly, there's a little matter of stealing from my employers.'

'Just a thought,' he laughed. 'I'm sure you'd make a fortune with some of Kassie's old thongs!'

The family football damage-limitation outing went off without a hitch. I mean, considering I don't know anything about football (though even I know more than Kassie), it was actually a bit exciting. We were in this executive box in the North Stand at the Spartacus ground. And there was all this lovely food laid on and a full bar – not that I had anything alcoholic, I was way too scared of messing today up. Imagine, getting papped whilst pissed? The kids loved it, Kassie was all over them – of course, there were cameras about – and they were lapping up the attention. And she was all over me, too, if I'm honest.

'Do you like football, then?' she asked me.

'Well, um, no, not really. I mean, I just haven't watched that much . . . but my brother's mad for it. He supports Man U.'

'Oh, well, I know it's not the right team but we'll have to get Brett to sign something for him.'

'Oli would love that!' I said, touched. 'Thanks, Kassie.' Looks like I'm going to be in little brother's good books for a while. I knew he'd be made up.

'Don't mention it,' she smiled, her eyes scanning the rows in front of us. Thousands of people in the stadium and she's trying to find the photo opportunity. But, as it happened, she's not as stupid as she sometimes seems. It worked.

The Perfect Match

The commitment of WAGs really knows no bounds. They tirelessly attend every game, while looking glamorous, and watch their menfolk shoot and dribble all over the pitch.

And while thousands upon thousands of fans hang upon every second of the 90 minutes of play, they too appear gripped on a more personal level.

Kassie Ballentine (28) and family turned out in force to watch husband Brett (28) play in last Saturday's exciting London derby. With a bit of help from nanny Katie Meredith (18), they managed to keep both Regan and Maximus entertained whilst following every nail-biting minute of the match.

Regan seemed to be following play quite well but little Maximus soon got bored and decided to play monkey along the railings and back to waiting Mum.

Kassie and Katie gossiped whilst keeping a close eye on the children. Kassie Ballentine's often accused of paying more attention to her shopping schedule than she does to her children, but on this occasion we say well done, Kassie. She couldn't have been a more devoted mum!

21

OK, I knew it was all too good to be true. Last night I heard the mother of all rows. I had my pyjamas on before bed, and had snuck down to the kitchen to get some milk – I'd run out and although I usually buy my own I didn't think anyone would mind if I took a cupful for my hot chocolate. I was coming back upstairs and had just got as far as Brett and Kassie's floor when I realized their bedroom door was open and there were raised voices coming out of it.

Cue Katie's usual hopelessness in high-stress situations. I was like, do I just bluff it out and walk loudly past their bedroom and up the stairs pretending I'm deaf? Do I tiptoe past and hope that no one comes out and catches me mid-tiptoe, which, knowing my luck, is highly likely to happen? Or do I remain where I am, clutching a mug of milk, listening to everything being said, getting more and more stressed, and simply unable to tear myself away from eavesdropping?

I told myself it was because I didn't want to get caught on my way past their room, but I have to admit, earwigging on other people's domestics is compelling.

Brett sounded off-the-scale angry. 'It's not the point, Kassie,' he was hissing. 'You lied to me then and you've been lying ever since. God, I'm even lying to myself.'

'You don't know what you're talking about,' Kassie virtually screeched. 'I wasn't lying, I genuinely thought I was.'

Was what?

'Oh, yeah, for about five minutes, just long enough to get that engagement ring on your finger, I should say. By the time we got married you'd been stringing me along for months.'

'I was confused,' Kassie's tone turned all innocent little-girl, 'that's all. I'd never been pregnant before.'

Brett even louder now. 'Yeah! And you still weren't! And you know it.'

'Oh, don't come the prude with me, Brett. It's not like I had to fight you into bed, was it? You knew who I was and you wanted me.'

Was I hearing right? Was Brett saying what I thought he was saying? Kassie had supposedly been pregnant when they got married and then all the press said she'd had a miscarriage but . . . apparently not, according to Brett. No wonder he was furious.

'OK, I admit it, Kassie, you did have a certain sordid appeal for a one-night stand. But that's all it should have been. A dirty little fling.'

I felt my heart starting to thump. This was serious.

'Well, if that's so, why didn't you leave me years ago?'

'I was going to, wasn't I, Kassie? But then you pulled the pregnancy trump card again, only this time it was true. God knows I love my kids, but sometimes when I think of the fact that you're their mother it really makes me sick.'

'You bastard!' she hissed. 'I've been nothing but supportive to you—'

'Supportive!' He was laughing at her now. 'Like I need your support, sweetheart. I'm the one with the career and the cash, remember. All your little "projects" – what do they amount to? Sweet FA. You've failed at everything you've ever tried to do. You were a failure when I met you and you're a failure now. The only decent things you've ever produced are those two little kids and you're too stupid to even appreciate that. You're even a failure as a mother.'

I could hear Kassie crying now and started backing down the stairs. I'd got about halfway down when I heard their door slam and Brett storm across the landing to the spare room.

I waited for what seemed like an eternity before I dared to venture back up the stairs. Everything was quiet now apart from my heart hammering in my chest.

My nan always says to be careful what you go nosing about for. You might not like what you find out.

I came home this weekend, after two sleepless nights. Hearing Brett and Kassie going at each other like a pair of deranged Rottweilers had really depressed me. It's such a mess between them. I'd managed to drag myself through the next day (let's just say Maxi had a bit more telly time than usual) and then today I drove down to Hastings. I just took the car, didn't bother asking if I could or not. They owed it to me, as far as I was concerned.

Usually it's really good to come home because I feel – well, I feel just that, so at home. But this time it was different. The only silver lining was time with Josh, but even that was a tricky one to get away with without fessing up to my parents . . . and frankly I wasn't really in the mood for more Katie-fuelled upsets in the Meredith household.

For a start, Auntie Chelle was in the dog house and no longer allowed to visit after her 'betrayal' (Mum's words not mine). Of course she strongly denies being the culprit, and frankly I don't really care, but Mum is absolutely indignant about the whole thing.

'How could she do that to you? That woman is so thoughtless/selfish/mean-spirited . . .' etc. etc.

I know she's trying to make me feel better but now my dad's sister has been completely ostracized and it's all my fault. I mean, I know ultimately it's her *own* stupid fault, but if I wasn't working for Brett and Kassie Ballentine . . . you get the picture.

So, it seemed hardly appropriate to mention the events of the past couple of days to anyone. Carly is in London, because she works Saturdays now, and there's no one else that I trust enough to share with. I mean, it's not like I think Nan or Mum would go rushing off to the *News of the World*, but after the whole Auntie Chelle fiasco, it's not a risk worth taking. I even had to have a long hard think about whether or not I'd tell Josh.

At least giving Oli the signed poster of the Spartacus team cheered me up. He was so made up. 'I'm going to support Spartacus as well as Man U now!' he said.

Mum is being really 'sensitive' around me. She knows something is up but she also knows if she doesn't pry too much she's got more chance of getting me to spill the beans. Fat chance of that. I'm beginning to question the whole thing, whether I even want this job any more. Is it really worth it when it makes everything else in my life so difficult?

The whole media thing is too much. I mean, Kassie is obsessed. She's either courting media attention and then complaining when she's got it, or complaining when she hasn't.

And then there's Brett's accusation. I've always been so convinced he was the rotten apple in that particular barrel but now I'm not so sure. OK, I'm really not mad on the way he speaks to Kassie. If he despises her that much he could always leave. But he does love his kids and . . . if she really had conned him into thinking she was pregnant, that's about as low as you can get in my opinion.

My head nearly bursting with all that was on my mind, I finally managed to sneak out today – Sunday afternoon – for a 'walk'. I met Josh down on the seafront. It was a freezing cold day and the wind was howling. We crossed over the road and headed for a café.

'You all right, Squeaky?' Josh teased me. 'You seem to have lost your squeak today.'

I sighed. 'It's just work. It's . . . it's complicated.'

'Wanna talk about it?'

I sighed again and smiled at him weakly. 'It's just . . . I'm . . . well, I'm not sure I can.'

He looked a bit confused.

'Confidentiality and all that.' I tried to make it sound like it wasn't anything personal but Josh looked a bit hurt.

'Look, Katie, you don't have to tell me anything you don't want to . . . you know, if you think you can't trust me—'

'No, no,' I interrupted him. 'It's not that.' But it was that, wasn't it? My job was so mental that it made me not even trust my own boyfriend. Which I suppose he was. I did trust him, didn't I? If I was prepared to trust him with my heart again, after all that had happened before, I should be able to put my faith in him not to let me down.

And now, back in London at the Ballentines', I am even more confused.

Josh had been so lovely and understanding when I finally decided to tell him about the argument and everything. 'They're just nutters, Katie,' he said. 'You wanna keep in the real world with me.' And he kissed me so gently I really did think for a short time that everything might be all right. But then we had to say goodbye, and after saying goodbye to Mum I felt sad I couldn't tell her about him and that my family didn't love the boy I loved. It was bad enough leaving him, and now I had to go back to a house full of people who seemed to have lost sight of love altogether.

As bad luck would have it, Mrs Ellis was there when I got back. She decided to take the opportunity to give me a big lecture about not leaving the kids' stuff lying around.

'I don't think I should need to point out to you that the children's possessions are your responsibility,' she said firmly. 'It's quite clear where everything belongs. If you really find it so difficult to keep on top of your duties, perhaps you're in the wrong job.'

Well, it was the straw that broke the camel's back. I just crumpled. I couldn't help it, I could feel the tears coming before I could stop them. And then something really unexpected happened. Mrs E started being really nice!

'Oh dear, Katie,' she stammered. 'I didn't mean to upset you. It's just, it's my responsibility to keep everyone in line . . .' She sort of reached out and patted my back. I think that was as close to being touchy-feely as she's ever going to get. And somehow that just made me feel even worse. Before I really realized what I was doing, I'd spilt everything out to her in a big gushy rush – even the stuff about overhearing Kassie and Brett rowing and how hard it was living in a goldfish bowl.

She was so sweet about it all.

'We all find it hard at times, Katie. But try to keep some emotional boundaries,' she counselled me. 'The Ballentines are your employers. You are here to look after the children, not to be their friend.'

I know that's true, but it's not that simple. When Kassie decides to be all matey with me, I can't exactly tell her to sling her hook, can I? She's the one with the boundary issues, if you ask me. I know she's lonely – though she'd never admit it. She lives this superficial existence, where people are constantly fawning over her, but no one actually likes her. They're just hoping for a handout, or a leg up the celebrity ladder, and they're using her.

I can't help feeling trapped here. The only thing keeping me going is the children; the rest of it is just too surreal. I didn't think it would be like this.

Still, Mrs E put things into perspective.

'It's not a life sentence,' she pointed out.

Which is true. I am allowed to leave if I want to. And there are plenty of jobs out there with less high-profile clients. If that's what I want.

It was as if Mrs Ellis read my mind. 'Don't you worry. The next few weeks'll be a bit easier. Kassie's diary's fully booked and Brett's got a really busy match schedule. So you just keep your head down and everything will be fine.'

Mrs E turned out to be right. The last few weeks have been relatively calm and normal here.

Kassie's been all over the country on her promotional tour – not that it seems to be doing much good, every review I've read of her video has slated it – and Brett is footballing his feet off. But best of all, Kassie's taken to phoning Maxi and Regan on a regular basis, which is way out of character, but I'm not going to knock it. And it makes the kids happy. Regan's so good on the phone – she's got the hang of having a conversation on it. But poor old Maxi, he keeps on holding up things he's made and saying: 'Look at this, Mummy!' Bless.

Hotline magazine 2007

KB's Top of the Flops

Yes, the Queen of Kitsch does it again in her spectacularly dismal fitness video. Like we need to take tips from a skeletal Barbie Doll who's taken one too many trips to the tanning salon. Let's face it Kassie, there's only one truly fit bod in your household . . . and it isn't you!

22

November already. My probationary period is over. I've sort of got over my paranoia and I really hope Brett and Kassie want to keep me on. Brett and I seem to have come to a mutual understanding: I don't want to be his mate and he doesn't want to be mine but we both respect the fact that we love the kids. Suits me fine.

As for Kassie, she's back from her promotional tour, but she's going out a lot. I have no idea why or where. When she is at home, she's reverted to a default mood of snappy and manic. The mood is down, I assume, to the fact that her workout DVD has absolutely bombed and she's been mocked by the tabloid press.

Kassie's also had another big bust-up with Creepy Ken, who is now threatening to sue her for loss of earnings or slander or libel or something. God, agents are a slimy, fickle lot. If it was me I'd tell him to stick it where the sun don't shine, but knowing Kassie, she'll be gearing up for one of her over-the-top making-up sessions with the creep.

Thankfully, now that I've actually got a life, I don't have to put up with it that much. I reckon Josh is getting a bit too comfortable in the lap of luxury, though – he's always suggesting we stay in, rather than go out drinking or clubbing. Never had him down as a homebody. Does this mean he's thinking of settling down? Gulp. I'm too young for all that yet, even if I have had the obligatory wedding and two-point-four-kids fantasy. Suffice to say, all my going out is done with Carly, Gemma and Leanne.

Carly's so loving living in Islington with the girls. I can see why – and I'm round there every spare minute not spent working, sleeping or seeing Josh. Never thought I'd say I prefer being crammed into a flat with two nurses, one bathroom, a dodgy boiler and a TV with only five channels to a swanky west London townhouse with all mod cons, but I do. I think it's known as a REALITY CHECK. Spending time with Regan, Maxi and Ted is fine, but I need to see people my own age every once in a while!

Leanne's quite petite with jet-black hair, loud and Scottish. And Gemma is a size-16-and-happy-with-it black girl with a 'mad weekend afro' (her words not mine) that she tames for work. Gemma has just got the best sense of humour – she works on a children's ward, so maybe she needs it. It really makes me realize how shallow my job is in comparison to the stories she tells. Some of those families go through hell and yet they all seem so brave and accepting. Gemma's really pragmatic about it. She's like: 'In the same situation we'd all do the same.' Somehow, I can't see Kassie not turning it into her own personal melodrama if one of the kids were ill.

It turns out that Gemma has actually met Lady K. 'She came to do a charity visit thing on our ward,' she told me the other night.

'Oh, right,' I said, surprised but not that surprised. I mean, Kassie never misses an opportunity to put on a caring face. OK, that's probably unfair. What I *should* say is good on her for taking time out of her busy schedule and raising the profile of those in need. At least I thought that until Gemma put me straight.

'Yeah, and she was a total cow. She was like "I can't drink the coffee it's disgusting and I might get MRSA and I can't touch anything or sit down for the same reason" and she was all holding hands and kissing children's heads whenever the camera was on her and then she was virtually wiping her hands and mouth with a disinfectant wipe the second she was out of shot – in front of the children and everything.'

For some reason I went red when she said that, as though Kassie's behaviour reflected on me. 'Oh, come on,' I said feebly. 'Surely she wasn't that bad . . . was she?'

Close-Up magazine 2007

Caring Kassie Brings Christmas Cheer to Sick Children

Caring Kassie Ballentine spread a bit of joy this week at a childrens' Hospital where she helped Santa distribute presents to seriously ill children. With toys galore and even a couple of signed footballs from her husband Brett's club, Spartacus, it was a bounty bound to make any child's Christmas complete. And even Santa looked chuffed as the blonde beauty – whose new underwear range, Kassie B, was launched earlier this month – sat on his lap and told him just what she'd like for Christmas. It seems he's already got what *he* wanted – and from the look on their faces, so have the little kiddies.

23

Having just got one bit of bad vibe sorted, I got back to a bit of good vibe. Well, I *think* it's good – but maybe it's just a bit too cosy too soon? Josh's going to be in London for a whole week! His firm normally puts them all up in hotels but he wondered if I maybe had 'a little space on my sofa'(!) for the odd night when he didn't fancy shacking up with the lads. Of course I said yes, but I made it clear there'd be no funny business going on. I mean, I want to be with Josh, but I don't want to lose my virginity to somebody I don't 100 per-cent trust yet. Josh did a bit of a faux-sulk on the phone when I said as much to him, but then said it was absolutely fine and of course he understood.

So Josh came over on Wednesday. He'd had Monday and Tuesday night out with the lads (which was fine by me: I saw Carly and the nurses on Monday, and last night had a lovely time with a face pack and a family-size packet of Maltesers) so he was looking a bit shabby.

I ran him a hot bubbly bath and sat on the side chatting to him as he soaked, admiring his well-toned arms and back, sleek with water. Resisting his charms was not going to be easy, I could tell, if he carried on flaunting his fit physique. Even Kassie, who doesn't notice anyone but herself in the mirror, commented on what a looker he was. 'Better hang on to him, sweetheart,' she said. 'It's not often you get that kind of body with a brain.' I'd be a bit insecure if I didn't know that she is so not Josh's type – he goes for the 'classier' kind of girl. That would be me, of course, ha, ha . . .

Anyway, Kassie is cool with him staying over, and Josh has made an effort to be friendly with her. I caught him chatting to her not long after he'd come round asking her if she needed him to build some more storage space for all her thousands and thousands of dresses, shoes and bags. Kassie was tittering like a Desperate Housewife. Talk about the Diet Coke ad.

'You're all right, darlin',' she said, giving his shoulder an unnecessary squeeze. 'I'm planning to give it all to charity anyway, but there just aren't enough hours in the day. I don't get a chance to sit down, let alone sort through my old tat!'

So, Josh and I got stuck into sampling domestic bliss. It was like playing at being married for a while, I guess. I was going to cook us some dinner after his bath (and my cold shower!).

'Are you happy, Josh?' I asked, swirling some bubbles between my fingers. 'I don't mean in a soppy way, just, with your job and everything, is it what you thought it would be?'

Josh knew what I was getting at.

'Yeah, mostly,' he said. 'I mean, it's different to you. My job hasn't got any of the . . . the complications. I turn up, I do it, I go home, I don't have to think about it again until I'm back in the van on my way to the next site. Fat Al gives me a bit of "constructive criticism" as he calls it every now and again, but the rest of lads are a good laugh, the money's not bad. And when I think about the alternatives . . . I guess I'm doing OK.' He sat up in the bath, causing a wave of water to slap back and then forward towards the taps like a mini tsunami. He looked at me intently. 'And that's you too, isn't it, Katie? I know your job's got pressures and stuff and it's hard at times, but you love the kids, right, and what are the alternatives? Some suburban family, or local nursery?' He looked around the luxury surroundings of my en-suite bathroom and snorted. 'I know where I'd rather be.'

'Yeah, s'pose,' I said quietly.

Josh blew a bubble off his arm. 'Now stop moping, girl, and get scrubbing my back!'

24

Kassie's still out most nights these days, and Brett's acting very strangely indeed. Not sure what's up with him, but the other night he was on his mobile in the study, which has two landline extensions in it. And he was kind of whispering into his phone. I heard it as I was coming up the hall. Yet again I was in prime eavesdropping position. However, I had learnt my lesson on that score, and this time I approached and knocked really loudly on the open door. Well, I don't know if I'm just imagining things, but he dropped that phone like it was red-hot and then looked really guilty.

'Oh, sorry,' I said cautiously. 'The children were hoping you could come and say goodnight.'

'Right. Yeah, sure.' There was a really awkward pause. 'That was just my manager fixing a session tonight,' he went on, indicating the phone. 'Busy day tomorrow. Big match, Liverpool, need to have our strategies in place.' Nervous laugh.

I think I was looking at him with an obviously suspicious expression, before I managed to rearrange it into something resembling interested. 'Yeah? That's great,' I said in a way-too-jolly voice. Brilliant! I should get a job as a spy; my covert operations skills are second to none.

I know Brett's got a busy schedule and everything, and granted, I don't know anything about football, but do footballers actually *train* in the evenings when they've already been at it all day? Because, like Kassie, Brett's been out A LOT recently. The other night Maximus asked him if he would be staying at home after he'd tucked him in and Brett was all flustered and said, 'Well, um, Daddy might have to go to training tonight.'

I was just outside Maxi's room at the time, folding some of his clean clothes on the chest of drawers on the landing, trying not to listen to their conversation. But then Maximus said, 'How can you train at night-time, Daddy?'

And Brett definitely sounded uncomfortable. 'Well, we've got lights . . . er . . . come on now . . . bedtime . . . night night.'

'But Daddy— '

'Can't talk now, son, gotta go, night night, sleep tight . . .' And then Brett kind of reversed quickly and softly out of the room, like he couldn't wait to get away from his son.

What was that all about? If I didn't know better I'd say someone's got a guilty conscience.

And then when Kassie finally got home later – I was in the kitchen organizing the breakfast things for the kids so I didn't have to do it in the morning rush – she said to me, 'Where's Brett?'

'He's at training,' I answered, trying to sound all innocent like I had no clue anything odd was going on.

And do you know what she did?

Arched her eyebrow and said, 'Oh.' And it wasn't an 'Oh, fine'. It was definitely an 'Oh, *really* . . . that *is* interesting.'

So there you go. It's not just me.

WAG Fever magazine 2007

Caught on Camera –
Shopping for Brett, Kassie?

Here's something you don't see very often: the never knowingly underdressed Kassie Ballentine out without an ounce of bling and carrying – not a Club bag that cost thousands, but one humble white plastic carrier bag like the ones you get from Poundstretcher! Has Brett put a ban on Kassie's cash? No, we reckon she was getting him a cheap little gifty to keep him sweet, whilst, you guessed it, leaving loads more ker-ching for her!

25

Surreal thing number eight hundred and sixty-three has just happened. Kassie has done one of her full three-sixty mood changes and all of a sudden I'm her new best friend again.

She's a bit like a goldfish. She's all bent out of shape over something and it's like the end of the world, and then something else comes along and takes her attention and previous gripe is completely forgotten about.

So she was mad at me over the nanny/bad-parent exposé, and then she was even madder over all the bad press her workout DVD was getting, but now she's all happy as Larry again because the launch of her special one-off Kassie B Underwear Christmas Collection is coming up and it's going to be like The Event of the Year! And she wants me to come along. Well, actually, she referred to me as 'rent-a-crowd' which is not exactly flattering, but I can't say I'm not intrigued to be consorting with the C List at Club It. So who am I to complain?

'We'll get you all kitted out, darlin',' she said to me. 'Get your hair and make-up sorted. No more plain Katie for you!'

Plain Katie? Thanks very much.

'Something short – show off those pins. And you'll have to be wearing Kassie B undies of course!'

Oh, of course. Did I have any choice?

The night was pretty awesome actually. From the moment we arrived it was like being on another planet. Planet Celeb. We pulled up after everyone else so that Kassie could make this grand entrance. And it was just like nothing I've ever experienced before. There were flashbulbs going off everywhere. I was attempting to get out of this car with some semblance of dignity when I realized there was actually a photographer lying in the gutter at my feet. 'He's going for the knicker shot,' Kassie reliably informed me with a wink. I'm not entirely sure what she meant but it didn't sound good. And as I can't even walk in the absolutely exquisite, but unfeasibly high, Jimmy Choos she'd forced me into, I'm sure he probably got what he came for!

Club It is amazing: huge rooms, little twinkly lights, fantastic sound system. There was hot and cold running booze and all these really sexy waiters and waitresses in Kassie B underwear handing out champagne and canapés. I felt completely out of my league. I also felt completely like I was having some kind of alien invasion experience as, although I was definitely still me, after the Kassie treatment I so wasn't.

My hair had been backcombed and bouffed into this huge up-do and I'd been sort of poured into a gauzy little silver dress with an amazing push-up bra underneath. My breasts had developed a sort of *Carry On* personality all of their own, and I tell you, they'd never felt quite so exposed or so precarious. I had on a pair of heels that were so high I was actually terrified to move in case I broke my ankle/ leg/neck, and I was wearing so much make-up I wasn't sure I could actually heave the sides of my lips up into anything even vaguely resembling a smile. 'Think Barbarella, darlin',' Kassie said. I think that's like some ancient Jane Fonda movie, but means nothing to me 'darlin'. Still, all in the name of employment.

I just sort of hovered in a dark corner watching everyone air-kissing and luvvying it up. Repulsive Creepy Ken was back in the fold again. I think they've got like one of those parasite/host set-ups going. Neither of them can actually live without the other, even though they drive each other mad and each blames the other as soon as anything goes wrong. Ken came over and checked me out. Well, checked my chest out.

'Don't you scrub up lovely?' he said. Well, it was more a sort of slurry sneer, but hey, I guess it works on some people. 'I could launch your career, baby. We could do something with those.'

Oh my God! I had to get away from this man.

'You take my card, baby. We'll talk.' He made a phone with his hand and then swung it forward into a pointing finger. Cool! Then he caught an even better pair of breasts in his beady eyeline and went off after them like a bloodhound on the trail of a fox.

'Don't call me baby,' I hissed at his back as he lurched off into the crowd. Ugh! I felt unclean even talking to him.

After that, I stayed rooted where I was for most of the night. Partly because it was a dark corner and no one seemed to notice me hiding there, and partly because I wasn't actually sure I could walk! It was amazing, watching everyone checking each other out – obviously terrified in case anyone happened to turn up in the same frock.

And then there was the main event of the evening – the catwalk show. All these girls with unbelievable bodies – tall and thin but with breasts that defy gravity – parading up and down in platform wedges while this high-octane music pumps out all over the place. I have no idea how they do it. I'd be head over heels in seconds. I have to say, some of Kassie's underwear isn't all that bad. I thought it was going to be kind of Ann Summers cheesy, but it's actually quite cool. Mind you, the bodies it was wrapped around could make anything look good.

And then comes the grand finale: the mystery model, star of the show everyone's been a-buzz about. And, like everyone else, I'm absolutely flabbergasted when it turns out to be none other than . . . Vixen.

Oh yes, *that* Vixen. Kassie Ballentine's arch-enemy and notorious Page 3 Stunna, Vixen Moriarty!

Kassie is so clever. If she can't nail publicity just on the back of the underwear itself, or even the celebrity bash, why not pull the one thing out of the bag no one would expect? Kassie and Vixen have had this long-running mutual slagging match going since goodness knows when and now, here she is as the star attraction in Kassie's show. I have to admit, although I have always regarded Vixen Moriarty's image as a touch on the tarty side for my liking, she's got an amazing body. She had these (nasty) platinum hair extensions scraped up into a high ponytail, but it made her eyes look huge and dark. I guess she's not known as a Page 3 Stunna for nothing with that figure, either. Kassie claims her boobs are fake and that naturally she's a 32 AA cup, but whatever they're made of they're pretty impressive. Vix was strutting along, wearing a bra and thong set that would have made anyone other than Kate Moss look like a cellulite-ridden old heifer. But she looked incredible. I reckon all those hours at the gym every day have more than paid off for Vix Moriarty.

Everyone got totally excited when she appeared. I guess because it was a shock – what with her and Kassie supposedly being arch-enemies. I've got to hand it to Kassie, she was so on form, circling round everyone and air-kissing to Olympic standard. Every now and then she'd circle by me, 'All right, darlin'?' and I'd sort of nod mutely.

Then, quite late, she said to me, 'Here, I know what would cheer you up,' and she made little sniffing gestures with her finger against her nose.

Was she saying what I thought she was saying? I could feel panic rising in my chest.

'You wanna bit of Kassie's magic powder?' she laughed. Come to think of it her pupils did look a bit dilated and it wasn't *that* dark in there.

'Nah, you're all right,' I managed lamely.

'Whatever, darlin'. See you later . . . Dale darlin', long time no see . . .' And she was off.

God, I felt like such a silly little girl. Was I ever out of my league. And out of my comfort zone. I checked my watch. Midnight. I decided to get out of there before Kassie came circling back round me again. I grabbed my coat from the cloakroom and pushed my way past a throng of identikit girls with ironed hair wearing what looked like slips and legged it on to the street to a conveniently waiting cab.

the Sun

Looking Good, Mr B – But What's the Missus Wearing?

Brett Ballentine was looking his usual cool self, immaculately turned out in an Armani suit and crisp white shirt at an awards party last week. But what the heck was his wife wearing? Draped in dodgy gold slacks, we have to wonder if poor old Kassie B got dressed in the dark. Can they not afford a decent mirror?

The pair barely spoke a word to each other all night and stayed on opposite sides of the room. Maybe Brett was too embarrassed to be pictured next to the scary pants of gold!

26

I nearly had a heart attack this morning. Talk about déjà vu.

I walked into the kitchen to find Kassie leaning up against the breakfast bar holding a newspaper and giving me the evils.

Oh God, what now, I thought, feeling very sick.

'Well, look at you, you saucy minx!'

She let out an ear-splitting cackle, which seemed to go on and on. She held the paper out to me and there I was, large as life. Well, actually, I should say there were my *knickers*, large as life. Kassie B Christmas Range knickers, granted, but still very recognizably attached to me. The photo had been taken when I'd tried, obviously not hard enough, to get out of the car in a lady-like manner when we arrived.

'I told you they was after the knicker shot!' Kassie shrieked with delight. 'Looks like they got it, eh?'

Yeah, hysterical. I couldn't be more proud. Not.

The Naughty Nanny's Wearing Her Boss's Knickers!

No, Katie Meredith (18), nanny to Brett and Kassie Ballentine's two children, hasn't been riffling through her boss's drawers (ooh er). She's merely seen sporting the latest in luxury underwear from the Kassie B Exclusive Christmas range. And what better way to support your boss than by wearing a pair of perfectly pretty pants? With a nanny like that, we bet the little Ballentines are as pleased as punch. And as for Brett . . . we couldn't possibly comment!

I waited for the inevitable phone call from home, and sure enough, an hour later, Mum was on the blower.

'Good Lord, Katie, what on earth got into you? Your nan nearly had a stroke. She's convinced you're on drugs. You're not on drugs, are you?'

I took a deep breath. 'Mum, for heaven's sake, calm down. Give me some credit! It was an unfortunate pap shot, that's all.'

'Pap shot? What on earth is that when it's at home?' Mum sighed down the phone. 'It just looks a bit . . . cheap, Katie love. I know you're a sensible girl, but it is a bit of a shock seeing your eldest daughter in a state of undress on the front page of the *News of the World*. Your dad doesn't know where to put himself, he's so embarrassed. He can barely show his face down the social club without some comedian making a wisecrack about it. I'm not sure he'll ever live it down.'

Poor Dad, poor Mum, poor me.

Ever get the feeling you've been set up? I think Kassie knew what was going to happen the moment she put me in a way-too-short dress and way-too-high heels. Still, it got her her publicity and as far as getting her own back for my last media outing – hey, it could have been worse.

U lk amzing! Gemma and Leanne are dead jel – where'd ya get those sexy legs!? x Cx ps – nice keks!

Squeaky lks sooo sexy – it's having a seriously bad effect on me. The lads on site can't believe you're my girlfriend. They are so jel. Can't wait to see more of your flesh, in the flesh. J The B

I suppose it's good that my mates have decided to celebrate that hideous picture, rather than read me the Riot Act, but I agree with Mum. It's beyond undignified. And frankly I'm disappointed in Josh's reaction. Isn't a boyfriend supposed to get all protective and indignant at the mere thought of anyone other than him seeing his girlfriend's underwear?

Particularly in such a cheesy pap shot. It's not like I'm modelling for La Perla, is it?

It was fun getting dressed up for that party, and yeah, it was fun doing some star-spotting, but flashing my Kassie B knickers to the nation? That's just mortifying.

Hotline magazine

VIXEN LOOKS FOXY IN KASSIE BALLENTINE'S KNICKERS

No, she hasn't been going through her arch-enemy's laundry. It seems the battling babes have decided to bury the hatchet (not in each other for a change!) and Vixen did a star turn at Kassie Ballentine's exclusive winter season underwear launch. Vixen (26), whose ample 32FF boobs need a lot of support, spoke very highly of her new chum's lingerie range. 'She's got some lovely stuff, really sexy. Honestly, I could hardly keep my hands off myself!' Steady on, girls – people might actually start thinking you like each other, rather than just needing the publicity!

27

I dragged myself, in sackcloth and ashes, back to Hastings last weekend. Predictably, Nan refused to come over, and Dad can hardly look me in the eye. As for poor old Oli, he just doesn't know what to do with himself. Jo's the only one in the family who's not shunning me. She's always seen me as her square saddo big sister, and I think now she's quite impressed at the new wild-child Katie she thinks is beginning to emerge. Er, think again, Joanna. In the unlikely event the opportunity ever arises again, I will not be getting my pants papped. I've learnt my lesson. My pants are now well and truly under wraps.

But the really good news is that I'm not spending Christmas with the Ballentines. Instead I've managed to wangle Christmas at home with the family and I'm not joining the Ballentines until the day after Boxing Day – and then spending a week up in Yorkshire.

Oh joy. Seven days holed up with the odd couple.

Still, I'm chuffed because maybe I'll be able to build some bridges with the Meredith clan – mainly Nan – over Christmas.

Kassie B and the Perils or Plastic!

Kassie Ballentine has a word of warning for anyone who thinks PVC trousers are a good idea. 'I have the sweatiest gusset in the room. I'm ashamed to reveal I actually have sweat dribbling out the bottom of these trousers!' My, that girl's a class act.

28

Well, Christmas was a right barrel of laughs. Ceasefire didn't exactly happen. Oli has bounced back, bless him, but Dad's still being all distant with me. And Nan can barely bring herself to be civil, or even actually speak directly to me. It's all done via Mum or Jo. 'Joanna, dear, could you ask Katherine if she could pass me the salt?'

Even Auntie Chelle has found another axe to grind, though as usual, it's totally self-serving. She seems to think I must now actually be best mates with Vixen Moriarty and that I could have given Lynette's modelling career a leg-up if I'd only made the effort. (The fact that I haven't actually met Vixen and that Lynette doesn't even want a modelling career is obviously irrelevant.) Poor old Mum, meanwhile, is floating around saying, 'Another mince pie, anyone?' in this falsely bright voice, in the vain hope that she can pour oil on troubled waters by pretending everything's just like it's always been.

I only managed to see Josh later on Boxing Day. He said he had to work right up to Christmas and that he'd got to spend Christmas Eve through to Boxing Day afternoon with all the rellies who are descending on the Markham household. His Uncle Will is over from Australia and his mum has been virtually blackmailing him not to leave the house.

I finally had to confess to Mum that Josh and I were sort of seeing each other again, and though she was hardly thrilled, she didn't kick off too much about it. Doesn't mean to say she approves of it, though. I know Mum, and I know that when she says, 'Seeing Josh, dear? Well, enjoy yourself then,' what she really means is 'How you could give the time of day to that cheating low-life snake, I'll never know.'

So, all in all, Crimbo was a bit of downer. When it was time to go on the 27th, I had a bit of tearful heart-to-heart with Mum.

'I'm sorry, Mum,' I said.

'What're you saying that for?' Mum soothed.

'The photo thing . . .'

'You've got nothing to be sorry for. Your nan and your dad'll get over it.'

'Yeah, but it made Christmas all strange, didn't it? I ruined Christmas.'

'No, you didn't, love. And Christmas is always a bit strange in this house, let's face it.'

'You don't think I'm letting my job get in the way, though?' I asked. 'Sort of putting it in front of my family? Not caring who it upsets?'

'Listen, love . . .' Mum looked over her shoulder, checking the coast was clear. 'To be honest, I think you were just unlucky with that picture. And if I was your age and had your job I'd make the most of it and to hell what Dad and Nan think. Honestly, Katie, you've worked really hard to get where you are. You enjoy it!'

I grinned. 'Thanks, Mum.' Then I returned to feeble mode. 'And Josh?'

Mum sighed. 'Oh, Katie, what can I say? You're a big girl now, it's not up to me to decide who's right or wrong for you.' She paused. 'I do find it hard when I think of how much he hurt you. You're my daughter and I'd do anything to protect you. But, you're a young woman now. I suppose it's time for me to let you make your own decisions. And if you're happy with Josh then I suppose I'm just going to have to accept it.'

I smiled again. 'I am happy, Mum.'

'Right then. In that case, next time you're back in Hastings invite him round for tea and we'll all let bygones be bygones.'

I was grinning from ear to ear and threw my arms round her neck. 'You know what, Mum,' I said into her neck. 'You're the best!'

Now Celebland (2006)

Got a Cold, Kassie?

We all know Kassie Ballentine likes the odd wild night out.
And judging from the way she stumbled out of the celebrity
bash held at the Royal Horticultural Halls this week was no
exception. But what's that mysterious white blob up her
nose? Agent Ken Mitchell says it's a cold sore . . . We
believe you, Kenny!

29

Well, I've made it to York station in one piece. Slumming it on the train! But Rex (the driver) was there to meet me so I got a bit of my swishy-status back. I was actually dreading getting to the house. If the last visit we had up here was anything to go by, it was hardly going to be a picture of peace, love and understanding. Although I had to admit I was looking forward to seeing the children. I'd missed them over Christmas and would've loved to have been there to see them opening their presents. Although I expect they got so many they were probably a bit overwhelmed.

Rex let me in. I was instantly nearly mown down by a remote control four-by-four hurtling towards me in the hallway. Say what you like about parquet flooring – it certainly lets you get the speed up in a toy car.

'Katie!' Regan came running towards me clutching her remote unit in her hand and nearly taking my eye out with the antenna. 'Maxi! Katie's here!' she yelled, jumping up towards me.

I crouched down to her level and wrapped her in a big hug. 'Wow! Is this what you got from Santa?' I asked as Maxi came hurtling down the hallway and knocked us both over, laughing hysterically.

And there we all were in a huge heap of cuddles and giggles when Kassie emerged from the living room.

'Get off the floor, Katie,' she slurred, clutching her champagne glass in her bony fingers. 'Remember your position, for God's sake.'

Kassie had been unbearable for days before Christmas, acting like a vile lady of the manor. Before I left to go to Hastings, she'd torn a strip off one of the maids, Julia, accusing her of nicking stuff. Said that loads of things had gone missing in the house. Julia was so upset that Mrs E had to intervene. It was nasty.

The children were still laughing and squealing, oblivious to their mum's frosty state, until she turned on them. 'You two!' she snapped. 'Be quiet, Mummy's got a headache.'

And then, when they carried on regardless, she grabbed little Maxi really hard by the wrist and really snarled in his face: 'I said, shut it.'

Then she turned on me. 'What?' she said. 'Has goody two shoes got a problem?' It was only midday and she already stank like a brewer's dray. I guess the pressure of being round the in-laws was really getting to her. Then she said, to no one in particular, 'I'm going to lie down,' and staggered off towards the stairs.

I picked myself up off the floor and did my usual 'Mummy's tired' routine to the children – funny how good I was getting at that – and guided them into the living room to show me the rest of their toys. Although inside I was already feeling really wobbly. A drunken, snarly Kassie was not the welcome I was hoping for. And it made me mad to see the way she'd talked to the kids. But it's not in my job description to judge, so I guess I have to just shut up and put up. For the sake of the children, I pasted that happy-happy look on my face and made like Mummy being the big old monster from Planet Sloshed was absolutely fine and dandy.

Brett had apparently gone out for a run, but Granny and Grandad were sitting, stony-faced, by the fire when I came in.

'Er, hello,' I ventured. 'Um, Kassie's just gone for a lie-down.'

I saw an exchange of looks pass between them and then they switched back to their usual super-dooper grampies mode, cooing over Regan and Maxi as they showed me their cars, robots, Gameboys, computer games and pile upon pile of chocolate coins. Santa had obviously been very generous that year. It almost seemed a little lame to give them the presents I'd got them. Although I hadn't bought them much, I really had thought hard about each of them before I'd got them anything. I went out to the hall to get my bag nearly tripping over Brett's running shoes that were lying by the front door.

I could see Brett's parents were quite pleased with my gift choices. I kept getting these approving little smiles. I know they worry about Regan and Maxi turning into totally spoilt little breadheads, so I guess my rather low-key and some might say old-fashioned gifts were right up their street.

Good to know there are at least a couple of people over the age of five in this family who actually might like me!

We were all sitting there enjoying watching the kids try and play a good old-fashioned game of Snap with their playing cards when Brett arrived back. It was maybe a bit odd that he came back in his car, but then I suppose out here in the country maybe you do have to drive somewhere and then go running? But what was *definitely* odd was that he was in jeans and a trendy T-shirt with his puffa jacket over the top; he had no sports bag with him; he had not a hair out of place and not a bead of sweat on his brow. I mean, I know he's fit but . . .

Still, I'm feeling quite kindly towards Brett at the moment as the next day he went off to this meeting at a local residential place for physically handicapped kids. It gives them adventure holidays and offers their parents some respite care. Apparently, according to Gramps anyway, Brett's really active on the board of governors and always puts in a personal appearance whenever he's in the area. He just gets on with stuff really quietly without any of the fuss and pomp that Kassie seems to need to make any of her worthwhile work seem worthwhile. Not a photographer in sight.

Uh-oh! Am I actually warming up to the Ice-man?

* * *

Another crap few days have gone by.

The kids are going stir crazy as the weather's been terrible. Brett's gone back to London as he's got a couple of matches on and he's training. Granny and Gramps have scarpered too – they obviously can't cope with being left alone with Cruella DeVil. Speaking of Kassie, she is in yet another stinking mood.

And then something else pretty weird happened. It was Brett's parents' last day with the kids, so Ted and I took them to the local farm park with Regan and Maxi. Ted and I were absorbed in watching this unfeasibly large pig rolling around in a big patch of mud when Maxi and Regan came running over and started jumping about in puddles next to us. We were shrieking and diving out of the way and trying to calm the two of them down when I noticed Granny and Gramps having a really earnest chat with this woman and her son.

The boy was maybe a year or two older than Regan, and the woman looked about Brett and Kassie's age. She was really pretty, slim with dark auburn hair and that amazing translucent, flawless skin. She had a really natural look – hardly any make-up on from what I could see. She was wearing dark jeans and a fitted jacket and a grey beret pulled over her reddish curls. She looked really good; stylish in a casually pulled-together way. She was holding on to Brett's dad's hand, talking really intently to him and Brett's mum. The three of them seemed so pleased to see each other and at one point Brett's mum let out this really heartfelt laugh at something the little boy said and she reached over and tousled his hair.

Ah, the penny dropped. This must be Beth, the sacred ex-girlfriend. I was totally intrigued, couldn't take my eyes off them. Ted on the other hand seemed to be taking it all in his stride, as if he was used to it. This obviously wasn't the first time Beth had collided with Brett's parents, accidentally or not.

Finally they all had this big group hug before Beth led her son away to a car up the lane by the farm exit.

We left it a minute or two, then Ted and I took the kids over to their grandparents. I swear I wasn't earwigging, but bits of conversation just couldn't help but drift over my way. 'Such a wonderful girl . . . and he's the spitting image—' But then Brett's mum suddenly noticed me coming towards her and immediately changed tack.

'Hello, dear,' she said brightly. 'We just bumped into a childhood friend of Brett's – catching up on old times.' And she and Brett's dad exchanged a kind of knowing look, before Grandad picked up Maxi and tickled him until Maxi squealed with delight.

So that was Brett's first love. I couldn't help thinking, a bit disloyally, that she and Brett would make a great couple. Really classy. Mind you, if she had a son older than Regan, it looked like she'd pretty much moved on too.

Kassie's Fashion Flaws

Kassie's given us some of her style tips – now get this.
'Firstly – don't let it all hang out, it's sexier to leave a bit to
the imagination.' Er, which bit, Kassie? And 'secondly, invest
in some timeless classics.' Pretty rich coming from the lady
who never wears anything twice!

30

Kassie's somehow managed to land herself a role as patron of some or other charity. When I asked her what the charity is, though, she seemed a bit nonplussed. 'D'you know, Katie, my mind's gone a total blank,' she said. 'Terrible, innit?' Anyway, point is she's decided to organize this huge celebrity fund-raising ball. Now, I hate to seem cynical, but the way she's going on about it you'd think this was more of a Kassie Ballentine publicity vehicle than a means of raising the profile of this charity – but hey, who am I to judge. And at least it's got her out of her hideous bad mood. There's only so much tiptoeing around someone you can do when you're under the same roof. And I like a motivated Kassie much better than the directionless misery she was at Christmas. The downside is that she and Ken are all pally again – apparently the whole Vixen thing was his idea. No coincidence that he represents Vixen as well as Kassie, but still . . . it worked and it's spurred Kassie on to bigger and better things apparently. And what's more, she seems determined to rope me into the action, too!

A Quickie with Close-Up Magazine

Kassie Ballentine (27) answers our quick-fire questions.

What do you wear in bed?

My engagement and wedding rings.

Who was your last argument with?

Brett, over whose turn it was to make a cup of tea!

What was the last text message you received?

From Ken, my manager, talking about an up-and-coming project.

Who are your three dream dinner party guests?

Brett – obviously. George Clooney – again obviously! And my real dad because he died before I was born so I never got a chance to know him.

What's your signature dish?

Beans on toast – I'm not the best cook!

Describe yourself in three words.

Misunderstood, kind and honest.

When are you at your happiest?

Slouched on the couch at home watching a soppy movie with Brett and the kids.

What do you most hate about yourself?

My temper – I can be bit on the fiery side!

31

Time is moving so fast at the moment. During the week, it seems that I have only just dropped Regan off at school when it's time to pick her up again. Must be all the little tasks Kassie is getting me to do in between – way outside of my job description, I might add. But, as I said, if it keeps her happy and not snappy then I don't mind. I just want harmony in the Ballentine house. Does that sound really goody two shoes? Can't believe I am so square these days. Give me an easy life over a rollercoaster any day, though. I'm not cut out for screaming matches and confrontation.

Often on a Friday Josh finishes early, and last Friday he helped me with the school run, Bless him, he knows how much I don't like driving in London! I caught Kassie in a good mood and she said it was fine as long as he didn't interfere with my time with the children once we got back home. Not a problem. He just hangs out in my quarters waiting for me to finish work – something he doesn't seem to mind too much, funnily enough!

I can't believe how much Regan's come on since starting school. She's gone from not really knowing any letters to knowing the whole alphabet, being able to write really brilliantly and being able to read lots of three- and four-letter words. Every day when she gets back from school after she's had her snack and her quiet time we do her school reading book together.

Sometimes, if she's a bit tired, she can't really be bothered to work out the words and she just guesses them – wrong, usually – but when she really concentrates she's dead good at working them out. Then I have to write a comment in her record book. I wonder how many other children only ever have comments written in by the nanny. Brett and Kassie didn't even make it to the last parents' evening. I didn't have to, but I went in their place. How can they expect the children to do well at school if they don't show an interest? Yeah, I know, I'm starting to sound like Super Nanny – like I'm some kind of authority on bringing up kids the right way. But it's difficult not to be disapproving of parenting skills like Kassie's. Brett, well he's got a bit more of an excuse, but Lady K does nothing but avoid being a mum to those two. Poor little mites.

Still, its not all starched apron and attitude for me. Last night Carly's salon were putting in a few entries at this hairdressing event – it's like the BAFTAs for hairdressers. Gemma, Leanne and I went along to support Carly, of course. I can't say that the free food and booze wasn't an enticement, not to mention that the venue was the Hilton!

The champagne flowed all night, and though I had decided to pace myself, I downed the first two glasses in no time, and had to fill up on the yummy canapés. Not that they amounted to much once they were in your stomach, but they stopped me from keeling over into the ornamental fountain, which was the important thing.

'This is the life, eh?' Gemma said. 'I bet you get to do this all the time, don't you, Katie?'

'As if!' I laughed. 'Most of my time is spent picking Play-Doh out of the carpet and mopping up after Maxi's little "accidents".'

Carly was backstage assisting with the 'creations' – apparently most of which were done with wigs. Not sure I get it, but what do I know? So me and the nurses were left to our own devices, which was fine by us as I think Carly was a little worried we wouldn't behave ourselves. I had no intention of disgracing myself – not after the whole 'knickers' fiasco. But Gemma and Leanne were certainly letting it all hang out, if you get my drift.

They are both outrageous flirts, and boy, can they knock it back. Every time a tray of champagne swished past us they grabbed another glass each. I couldn't have kept up with them if I'd tried – they're in a whole different league to me. Bona fide party girls, those two.

'Come on, Katie,' Gemma laughed, pointing with her empty glass at my full one. 'Get it down your neck.' She nabbed a waiter. 'Three more, por favor!' She launched herself at the tray and thrust another glass into my other hand. I didn't want to seem like a total party pooper, so I showed willing. I took a couple of gulps of my third glass of champagne, and all of a sudden the warm glow of alcoholic fuzziness crept up on me. I wasn't drunk yet, but if I didn't stop then, I would be, soon. Dangerous.

Fortunately for me, once the actual show got started we were all expected to sit soberly at our tables. Carly came and joined us.

'No heckling,' she hissed.

'We wouldn't dream of it,' Leanne said in mock offence. I just smiled dopily and hoped I was doing a good impression of someone who was already a bit gone and didn't need any more booze, thank you very much! It wasn't that much of an act. Pathetically, two and a half glasses of champers were all it took to get me woozy. Must have been the lack of food.

After the show the wine started flowing again, and as Carly's salon had won second prize in some far-out category – 'Best barnet for going to the races' or something – they were all in very jolly frame of mind and I couldn't not have another drink, or two. Anyway, frankly, short of falling off a chair (twice) and encouraging Gemma to have a major snog sesh with a junior stylist from some other salon (can't even remember his name, or what he looks like) the whole evening is a complete blur.

I vaguely remember having an intense conversation with Gemma and Leanne, plus a couple of other people I didn't know. Haven't a clue what I was talking about – rubbish probably . . .

* * *

Talk about a rude awakening.

Carly stayed over last night after the do. She seemed full of beans this morning – probably because all the running around she was doing meant she didn't get the chance to drink anything. Lucky her. I felt like someone was swinging a mallet against my skull when I woke up. I can't believe what a lightweight I am these days.

And Carly didn't waste time filling in any blanks I had from the night before. I wish she hadn't told me. Ignorance is bliss, isn't that what they say?

'You were pretty chatty last night,' she said, slurping tea way too noisily for my poor head. 'What was all that stuff about Kassie's pregnancy?'

I sat bolt upright. Suddenly I felt wide awake. 'What?' I hissed. 'Carly, tell me you're joking.'

Carly shook her head apologetically, and took another slurp of tea.

'Oh. My. God.' I flopped back down and buried my head in the pillow. I was so fired.

'Honestly,' Carly soothed. 'I wouldn't worry, you were virtually incoherent. It's only because I know you so well that I could make any sense of it at all. And anyway, everyone else was trolleyed. Way more than you. I shouldn't think anyone remembers a word you said.'

'God, I hope not,' I whimpered. 'Because if they do my life is so over . . .'

'So?' Carly went on.

'So what?'

'Are you going to tell me or not?'

I still looked at her vaguely.

'Are you going to tell me what the whole "Kassie fake pregnancy" thing was about?'

I looked around the room, still not totally convinced that it wasn't bugged. Then I talked in a whisper. 'I heard them arguing, Carly,' I said.

'Oooh,' she said, laughing. She clocked my ashen face and bit her lip. 'Sorry. Not funny.'

'Yeah, it totally wasn't funny, Carls, honestly. It was nasty. And Brett . . . Brett basically said that she'd conned him into getting married by pretending to be pregnant.' I shivered. By now the room felt freezing cold to me.

'But she had a miscarriage,' Carly said, nonplussed. 'It was in all the papers.'

'Yeah, well,' I sighed. 'I think we both know that just because something's in the papers, it doesn't necessarily mean that it's true.' I flopped back on the bed and groaned. 'If it gets out that I've blabbed about this, there will be all hell to pay. I mean, Kassie was psychotic enough about the whole "unfit mother" article in the papers last time, which, let's face it, is small fry compared to this bit of gold dust. Not only would I lose my job, but I'd be unemployable. Who wants a nanny who can't keep her trap shut?'

'Don't worry,' Carly said unconvincingly, giving me a hug. 'It'll be fine. I'm sure it will.'

Heat 2007

Kassie and Vixen – A United Front!

Spotted at the TV awards Kassie Ballentine put in an appearance before disappearing for dinner at the Dorchester's China Tan restaurant with new bessie mate, Vixen. The amount those two eat, that's gotta be one tiny meal!

32

So far, no repercussions from my dreadful indiscretion the other night. I'm waking up every night panicking about it, mind you. But maybe, just maybe Carly is right and no one remembers what I said. And I don't like to tempt fate, but the mood in the house is decidedly up at the moment. Kassie spends most of her time in the study holed up with Creepy Ken, plotting, scheming and planning for the big ball. Brett's busy on (and apparently off) the pitch and we hardly ever see him – although he does make the effort to be around most bedtimes for the kids. And he seems to be mellowing a bit more towards me. It's like he knows me a bit better, and, dare I say it, he's beginning to trust me. Who knows?

Practically every weekend Brett takes the kids up to see his parents in Yorkshire. And Kassie doesn't even seem to notice, let alone mind. She acts like Brett's doing her a favour because of her charity ball coming up. She is so excited about it that nothing else seems to register with her.

She's all, 'Thanks, babe, yeah, I need the head space, you know what I mean, got loads of stuff to organize . . .' Then, straight back to studying lists of celebs who've been invited, working out who's coming and who's not and who to sit next to who. Fascinating stuff. It keeps her off my back, though, and for that I am truly thankful.

I tried asking her again about the actual charity cause, and got another totally typical Kassie response.

'Well, it's raising money for research into a disease, innit.'

'Right. What disease would that be then?'

She looked at me like I was stupid. Yes, like *I* was stupid. 'The sort of disease that makes you ill, Katie!' she said, beginning to sound exasperated.

'Yes, I realize that.' I was trying not to sound condescending. 'But is it like slowly degenerative, is it terminal . . . Has it got a name?'

'Oh, yeah, hang on.' She paused and I could virtually see the cogs turning in her brain. 'Multiple psychlorosis, it's called. I've got the stuff about it here.' She grappled in her huge leather bag, muttering away, 'As diseases go it's pretty much got it all . . . now, where did I put—'

'Multiple sclerosis?' I suggested.

Kassie stopped searching, and smiled in relief. 'Yeah, that's right, Katie. What I said. Multiple psychlorosis.'

Brett's in the papers more than Kassie at the moment, which is a bit of a turn up. There's this whole transfer-deal rumour thing going on. Trust me, I wouldn't have a clue about it, but every time I've been home for the weekend Oli's on my case: Is Brett going to Barcelona? Are they really going to pay twenty million for him? If he goes will I be going too?

I'm like, 'I'm only the nanny, not his manager. How the heck should I know?'

And Kassie's letting it all float over her head, as usual. The only time I overheard them coming even close to talking about it, she said, 'Yeah, babe, sounds great. Bit busy now though, babe . . .' Honestly, she needs to get IT'S ALL ABOUT ME printed upon a T-shirt. It would save everybody so much time in the end.

Kassie's so busy she even gave me tickets for Armond Giancarlo's show for London Fashion Week. I went with Carly, of course, but to be honest we were a bit out of our depth. It's all so luvvy. The show was impressive but it's the standing around chit-chatting after that gets us – it's all so fake. We'd rather just go to a bar somewhere where they had some music. And it was a bit scary: there were these animal rights activists there because Giancarlo uses real fur in his collection. I tell you what, I'm on the side of the foxes and the bunnies. Give me the old fake-o (fur-wise) any day. And me and Carly were trying to push our way through the throng before the bags of flour started flying. I tell you, I've had my share of the media limelight, and it's exit stage-left without a single flashbulb going off for me!

The Sun 2007

WILL BARCELONA WARM UP THE ICE-MAN ?

Brett Ballentine's got every right to look pleased with himself. But as per usual the top Spartacus striker's giving nothing away. With a rumoured twenty-million-pound transfer deal with Barcelona in the offing, he could soon be off to sunnier climes. But if the thought of playing football for the hot-blooded Spaniards is exciting him in any way, as always he's much too cool to show it!

34

Sunday Gossip – Exclusive!

Kassie B Didn't Miscarry

In a sensational new twist in the Ballentine family saga, a source close to the celebrity couple claims that Kassie B did not miscarry their first child. In fact, the *Sunday Gossip* can exclusively reveal Kassie Campbell (as she was then) was never actually pregnant with the baby she claimed to lose a few years ago. It was a lie. Designed to catch Brett Ballentine hook, line and sinker. Well, it looks like it worked. Callous Kassie made the whole thing up. 'She'll do anything if she thinks it will progress her career, or make her more money,' our source divulged. It seems while the nation mourned with her, Kassie was laughing behind our (and Brett's) backs. We knew you were low, Kassie, but SHAME ON YOU.

Well, it's finally out there – and it's only a matter of time before Kassie traces it all back to me. She is going absolutely

179

ballistic about the revelation in the *Sunday Gossip*, screaming down the phone at Ken for about two hours. She's threatened to rip his balls off – and that's verbatim, the whole street heard her say it! – if he doesn't find out who leaked the story to the press.

This might be a good time to change my name and leave the country, because I am so dead.

Having endured a morning of slammed doors and yelling on the phone, I just had to get out. I phoned Carly from the little park at the end of the road, which probably wasn't the best thing to do in my state of paranoid anxiety, and now we have just had the most massive row.

Basically, I sort of blamed her or Gemma or Leanne for selling the story to the *Sunday Gossip*. Well, who else can it be? I'm pretty sure Kassie wouldn't have told anyone. I'm the only one who overheard the argument and I'm the one who let the info slip at Carly's do.

Carly went mental. And I don't suppose I can blame her.

'God, you've turned into some kind of paranoid headcase,' she screamed down the phone. 'Is that what you really think of us? Me, especially? I've been your best friend for years, Katie. Do you really think I'd sell you out? You're unbelievable.'

'I don't want to believe it, Carly. I mean, I don't believe it of you, but Gemma and Leanne . . .' I felt like a cow saying it, but my job, my reputation, everything I'd ever worked for was hanging in the balance. 'I don't know what to think. I mean, where else could they have got the information?'

'I don't know,' Carly yelled. 'And I don't care. I don't give a shit about that stupid family and their stupid dramas. Not like you. You care more about your bloody precious Ballentines than you do about your real friends. Well, you stick with them, mate, and good luck to you!' And she slammed the phone down.

Boy, have I messed up on every level. I got drunk and blabbed really personal secrets about my employer. And now I've managed to lose my best ever friend into the bargain. And when Kassie finds out, all hell is going to break loose. Nice one, Katie.

At least there's one person who doesn't judge me. In contrast to Carly, Josh has been totally supportive again. I saw him last night – I lost it a bit after the row with Carls, and phoned him and he came over as soon as he could. Talk about a knight in shining armour!

'It's not your fault, Katie. It's the nature of the job. You must feel like you can't trust anyone completely. Carly should understand that.'

I sniffed. 'Yeah, but I virtually accused her – my best friend! What sort of friend am I?'

'Look, if you accused me, I'd understand it . . . I mean, you told *me* didn't you?'

I looked up at him, my eyes blurry and stinging with tears. 'But you wouldn't . . .'

'No, I wouldn't,' he said calmly. 'Of course. I wouldn't. He smiled and pulled me closer to him. But, if you felt the need to ask me, to make sure . . . I'd understand. Poor Katie, come here.'

He pulled me into a warm, velvety kiss and just for that moment everything seemed an awful lot better.

Now *2004*

No, we can't believe it either. It seems Kassie Ballentine really has come out wrapped in an old shredded curtain. Whatever next? The front-room rug perhaps?

34

Every day I am waiting for the call up, the caustic accusation, but it never comes. Amazingly it still hasn't occurred to Kassie that I could be the culprit. That's odd, considering the way she and Brett were yelling at each other the night I found out her secret. But then again, when you're as self-absorbed as Kassie can be, maybe you forget about little things like keeping your big mouth shut when virtual strangers are around. Well, that theory suits me, anyway. I'm just trying to keep my head down and get on with work and make myself as unnoticeable as possible.

Good job it's Easter, too. Apparently last year the Ballentines went to Yorkshire and had this brilliant Easter egg hunt with Brett's parents. Don't think that's on the cards this year, though. When I asked Brett if we'd be going up, he muttered something about Kassie not being keen (figures!) and that he'd be up there, but he was playing all weekend and it might be easier all round if the kids stayed in London with me and Kassie where they wouldn't get upset at him coming and going all the time. Strange logic, but who am I to argue? I am relieved that I'll be nearer Josh, anyway. I'm feeling a bit too vulnerable to be trapped in a stately home with crazy Kassie just at the moment.

The kids just loved their Easter egg hunt. We decided to bring it forward from the Sunday, as the weather was so good on Friday and Saturday. It was the first really spring-like weekend of the year so we had a picnic lunch in the garden. Ricardo had made loads of yummy sandwiches, and on Good Friday the kids and I had made chocolate crispy cakes – although I have to say a lot of chocolate went down their throats before it ever got anywhere near a crispy. I tried to make them eat some fruit before they stuffed all the cake and chocolates down themselves, but I have to admit it was a pretty futile task.

We spent most of Friday and Saturday in the garden running off all the chocolate, and clambering over their state-of-the-art climbing frame and play centre. I tell you, most playgrounds look pretty underequipped compared to Maxi and Regan's back garden.

It started to cloud over on Sunday morning and the temperature plummeted that British springtime way – you've no sooner whipped your cardi off with wild abandon because it's really sunny and hot than a cloud comes over, it's absolutely freezing and you have to make a run for the house and the central heating!

Anyway, I had another treat in store for the kids. I knew Brett had told me he was playing a match on Easter Sunday and Riccardo had said that most kick-offs were at 3 p.m. so

I thought we could find Daddy on the telly and have a little watch. The kids don't watch their dad playing football very often – Maxi is still too young really and even Regan struggles to stay interested for a whole game. But I thought they might quite like to watch for a little while so that they could tell Daddy they'd seen him do his stuff.

But of course, I'm such a dimwit when it comes to football and to finding anything on the hundreds of channels the Ballentines have got that I was completely unable to track down Spartacus anywhere. So we watched . . . you guessed it – *Cinderella* instead!

The News of the World

Spartacus Locked in Negotiations with Barcelona

Top striker Brett Ballentine is such a catch, it seems that even with a twenty-million-pound price tag, Spartacus are reluctant to let him go. But watch this space: Barcelona haven't given up hope of securing north London's golden boy. And with excellent shops and plenty of opportunity to top up her tan, we're sure Kassie Ballentine will be up for the move too. Although an insider close to the couple says she couldn't even master *gracias* on her last trip to Spain! But after the recent revelations about her miscarriage lies, we wouldn't mind if she learnt to say *adios*!

35

I actually banged into Brett in the hallway when he got back last night. Sometimes I'm such a lamebrain. I thought, Oh I know, I'll make conversation about trying to find the match and being all channel-challenged, but his reaction was totally weird.

I said, 'Hi, Brett.' See how chummy we are now? 'How did the matches go?'

'Yeah, fine,' he smiled back at me.

'We tried to watch Sunday's match,' I said, 'but I'm a bit useless with the Sky thingy and I couldn't find it. I thought the children might be quite excited.'

Brett gave me this really funny look – he sort of narrowed his eyes suspiciously for a minute, before he pulled himself together.

'Oh, right, yeah, never mind,' he said quietly, and he started heading off to the stairs. He was halfway there, when he stopped and added over his shoulder, 'Actually, I think they're still a bit young for it. They get pretty bored . . . perhaps it's better if you don't try to get them to watch it.' And that was it. Off up the stairs he ran, leaving me feeling like a right plonker.

I *know* they're too young for a whole match. I was only going to let them watch a little bit. I was *trying* to be nice.

Weirdo.

Closer (2007)

Spotted – Kassie Ballentine in cut-offs and slouchy boots on the King's Road.

36

This weekend I went home and set out on a long walk along the seafront, from one end of town to the other. It's an excellent way of clearing my head, I always find. Josh was away on a football weekend with a load of mates, so I was alone, but that was fine by me. Staring out to sea at the fishing boats and the groyne at one end, the pier, and the rocky outcrops – where I once actually saw a seal! – at the other, and the view across to Beachy Head in the distance. It was just so familiar and comforting. It's a magical view.

At least Jo seems to be coming out of her moody phase. She's actually working really hard, my mum says. Jo's the academic one in the family – and she wants to be a vet. I feel dead proud of my little sister, and we actually managed to have an adult conversation last night when I arrived. Jo is growing up at last. Wish I felt like I was. But pretty soon, being back in Hastings reminded me of Carly, and thinking about Carly made me feel bad.

I haven't actually made any plans to meet any mates, not even tonight, on a Saturday night. I can't bear the thought of them asking about Carly. And if she's already spoken to any of them they'll probably blank me anyway. No doubt she's told them what a cow I've been.

So it's a night spent in the bosom of my family, I guess.

Oli's still on at me about Brett's career. 'I think he should go to Barcelona,' he said to me at breakfast. 'A spell in a big European club is always good for a footballer's career.'

'Hmm,' I replied. I didn't want to squash him completely but I wasn't going to give him the idea I'm too bothered about Brett's career move. Oli would have been all over me like a football trivia rash. I mean, yes, I am slightly interested in the prospect of a move to Barcelona – Spanish guys are quite high on my list of fanciable fellas – but unless I hear it from the man himself, I'm not going to hold my breath. But Oli wittered on regardless and in the end I was forced to put down my magazine and actually pay attention. 'Actually, Oli, I did try to watch Brett playing recently. On Easter Sunday.'

Oli smirked at me. 'Yeah? Don't try and humour me, big sister. He didn't play on Easter Sunday.'

'Oh,' I said. 'What, was he on the bench or something?'

'Duh?' Oli groaned, obviously getting frustrated with what a complete and utter non-starter I am on the footy front. 'Spartacus didn't play on Sunday.'

'Yes, they did,' I protested. 'Leeds or Manchester or someone – a northern club. Newcastle maybe . . .'

Oli snorted. 'Read my lips, Katherine. Spartacus had one match at Aston Villa on Friday and then nothing else for the rest of the Easter weekend. Trust me.'

'But Brett said . . .' I started before trailing off.

'God, you live with Brett Ballentine and you still haven't got a clue. Why are all girls so football-backwards!' Oli shook his head and rolled back on the couch in disbelief.

I was very confused. I felt sure Brett had said he had matches all weekend, and if he hadn't, why had he spent the whole weekend away when he could easily have got back from Aston Villa? And anyway, when I'd told him I'd tried to watch the match he hadn't tried to correct me. I was starting to get an anxious feeling in my chest. Something was definitely going on with Brett, and whatever it was, I wasn't sure that it was going to be good.

Close-Up on the Stars!
Clothes on the Couch

Kassie Ballentine

Diagnosis

Kassie B looks more like a flashback from her pole-dancing past than a queen of the footballing scene. With other WAGs getting big ticks on the style front, Kassie's stepped out in this truly terrible canary-yellow, sequinned, tasselled dress. Her bag and shoes also clash with the dodgy frock. Is that Brett I see running for cover?

Prescription

I've tried my hardest but there's nothing redeemable about
this look – just bin it! Kassie, you've got such a lovely face –
why not let it outshine your outfit, rather than the other way
around? A more demure frock in a less lurid shade would
ensure cameras flashing for all the right reasons!

37

This weekend was Maxi's birthday party. Like everything else chez Ballentine, it wasn't exactly run of the mill!

That'll be because his parents aren't that interested in their kids' lives at the moment. Obviously with Kassie that's an ongoing situation. Brett is usually a bit more involved, when he's got the time anyway. It's no surprise that neither of them know who any of his little friends are. So it's up to me to make a list, with Maxi's help. Spending so much time with him, I know who most of his buddies are at nursery, and I know their parents, or their nannies, as I've made a point of introducing myself. It's easier anyway, if I do the inviting as, if Kassie took it upon herself to do it, most of them would be too freaked out, or horrified, to let their little darlings anywhere near Maxi's family. They know her by her reputation, of course, but in the flesh, well . . . Kassie's a bit of an acquired taste for the average human being.

There's also a playgroup I go to with him every now and again and there are a couple of little girls that he's taken rather a shine to there, so I've invited them too. Plus Regan's best friend from school, Spike.

'So,' I said, having run my provisional plan for the party past Brett. 'I was thinking of Zoom-a-Zoom as a venue. Do you think that would be OK?'

And Brett, who'd been staring into the middle distance all the while I was talking, was just like, 'Yep, fine, whatever you think's best, Katie.'

So that was it. Zoom-a-Zoom (which is like a trendy kids' café with a big soft-play climbing area) and a magician. Perfect for a four-year-old, I reckon. You're meant to have fifteen children or more to get the place to yourself. We only had seven kids but Brett paid the rest to keep it an exclusive do. Kassie had been totally absorbed in her own stuff and had given me the brush-off every time I tried to discuss Maxi's party with her, and yet when it came to the big day she was all, 'Oh, is this the best venue we could get?' If it had been left to her she'd probably have booked China White in town – with champagne and cocktails and a whole crew of *Hello!* photographers. Inappropriate, much!.

At least Brett made the effort to go down to Hamleys – after hours, naturally – and got Maxi a fantastic Scalextric mega-huge eight-lane Monte Carlo, metres and metres of track racing set and a load of other gear: designer clothes (very important when you're four) and some PlayStation thing. I got him some guinea pigs! Maxi loved the Scalextric – for about an hour, until it got too much for him – but I have to say, if you were to press me on the subject, he definitely liked my present best!

Like I said, the party itself was a bit surreal. It's quite

funny watching people trying to appear completely unfazed by the fact that they're in the room with two of the country's most talked-about celebs. The posh Knightsbridge types just went into snob mode (we're old money, therefore we're better than you anyway) and the nannies just stuck to chatting about the kids and helping to pass the plates of sandwiches around whilst, every now and then, having a good old gawp at Brett and Kassie.

Then the magician (the Marvellous Marvo) did his show, which was fairly naff but the kids absolutely loved it – they got a really rubbish balloon animal each, so why wouldn't they? Marvellous Marvo kept getting Maxi and Regan up to help him, which was very sweet. Maxi was obviously nearly bursting with delight over all of it. Brett was recording the whole thing and genuinely beaming at times, whereas Kassie was somewhere over the other side of the room fiddling with her phone and twitching because she couldn't have a fag inside the venue. There was no way she was going to lower herself to standing on the street like the rest of the faggy populace, but nicotine withdrawal put her in one of her stinkers, of course. Can't the woman even spare five minutes to look interested on her son's fourth birthday?

The pièce de résistance was Kassie's idea for the party bags. She'd ordered them from some swanky bespoke company and a lot of kids went home that afternoon with the latest state-of-the-art mobile phones, Internet-connectable Tamagotchis, and mini Armani T-shirts. My nan is going to have a fit when I tell her. If I'd had my way, a bag of sweets, a colouring book and a bit of crappy plastic tat would have done the trick, but then, I'm not Kassie. Thank God.

Now that Maxi's four, he'll be starting school in September. I guess I'm going to have to have a chat with Kassie and Brett at some point about how my job's going to change. Once Maxi goes to school full time, I'm going to have most of the day to myself. I almost wish Kassie would have another baby so that I definitely get to stay for at least a few more years . . . On second thoughts, considering the sensitivity of that particular issue, maybe that's not such a great idea.

38

I'm in shock. I got home yesterday afternoon to find Mrs E loading her belongings into a van outside the Ballentines' house. The look on her face practically turned me to stone, so I didn't dare ask her what was going on. Instead I tiptoed past her and into the house, where Kassie was pacing the hall, smoking like a dervish, ready to give me the full story.

'I've fired her,' she said, jerking her head in the direction of the front door. I hadn't even opened my mouth before she went on self-righteously, 'Conniving, deceitful old bat! Just shows you, Katie. You can't trust nobody!' She stubbed her fag out angrily in the plant pot on the hall table. 'Good riddance an' all, if you ask me. Always looking down her nose at me, she was.'

Apparently it was Mrs E who'd blabbed about Kassie's phantom miscarriage to the tabloids. Mrs Po-Face clearly wasn't above selling her soul to the devil, then.

Kassie had been apoplectic when she'd found out. Predictably it was Creepy Ken who'd given her the good news. He'd been on to some old pal at the newspaper trying to trace the source of the story and that's when it came out.

It had all been done over the phone, his friend said, but it was definitely a Mrs Ellis who'd supplied the story. It seems odd to me though, considering how cosy Mrs E is with Ken. And it doesn't seem quite her style, come to think of it. But at least it puts me in the clear. Honestly, 'relief' doesn't even begin to describe what I felt as Kassie sniped on about the treacherous housekeeper she'd 'always looked on as a mother figure'.

But after the initial euphoria had passed, I began to feel guilty. It could still have been me who was responsible for the story getting out. I mean, I told Mrs E as well as Josh and Carly about the argument I'd heard. If I hadn't done that . . . And then there was Carly. I felt gutted about blaming Carly. How could I ever have doubted her?

Kassie got all Mrs Ellis's stuff and literally threw it out of the house. Mrs Ellis didn't say a word; she totally ignored Kassie, who was screaming like a banshee that Mrs E was a dried-up backstabbing old witch who was bitter and vindictive. God knows what the neighbours thought. I hid up in the playroom pretending to put all the picture books into alphabetical order, but it was impossible not to hear every poisonous word.

Tantrum over, Kassie went into full throttle doing some fire-fighting over her dented image. When the story first broke she tried to keep a dignified (never thought I'd put that word with Kassie, but there you go) silence. But now she's desperate for some positive press. She's been on to Ken about plugging her latest project, the big charity ball, for all it's worth. And she wants him to do a story about her painful betrayal by a trusted member of staff and how she's been hurt to the core. She's priceless.

Sunday Mirror

KASSIE BALLENTINE — EXCLUSIVE

The Ultimate Betrayal

A tearful Kassie Ballentine has talked exclusively to the *Sunday Mirror* about her painful betrayal by a member of staff. Mrs Enid Ellis (60) had sold the story of Kassie's alleged phantom miscarriage for an undisclosed sum, thought to be up to £50,000, to the *Sunday Gossip*, despite years of supposed loyal service.

'I thought of her as the mother I never had,' Kassie sobbed. 'But it turns out she was just another person out to hurt me. The time I thought I was pregnant was very confusing for me. We had announced the pregnancy really happily to the press before I realized I'd actually made a mistake. I was so embarrassed, it seemed easier just to say I'd lost the baby. Of course, looking back, I realize how silly that was, but I was young and naïve and had no idea of the vicious nature of the press and supposedly trusted staff.'

Ex-pole dancer Kassie (28), who is often vilified for her nightclub antics, speaks quietly of her tireless work for charity. 'Everyone's very quick to point the finger when I do something wrong but what about all the good I do? My charity ball for instance – I hope you guys from the press will all be just as quick to cover that.'

Well, Kassie, the *Sunday Mirror* certainly will, and we have already made a pledge to donate £1,000. And it was worth it to see a smile on Kassie's face for the first time today.

39

This term's nearly over already. Regan's been in school for nearly a year! And Maxi is going to be starting in a couple of months' time. The weather's gorgeous and the kids are spending loads of time out in the garden. The end of the summer means I've been in this job a whole year. I can't believe how much I've come to love the kids in that time. My contract only runs for another year – honestly, it makes me well up even thinking about not being with Maxi and Regan any more. Pathetic or what?

We were out in the garden the other day and Brett came out and joined us. Regan and Maxi, of course, were absolutely delighted. They love it when Brett gives them a bit of time – which, to be fair, is getting more often now that the football season's drawing to a close.

They were playing a version of chase which simply involved them running round and round the garden shrieking when Brett came and sat down on the picnic blanket next to me – feigning exhaustion. A likely story. Excuse me, but don't you usually spend ninety minutes running up and down some enormous field in pursuit of a smallish spherical object? I hardly think fifteen minutes chasing a four-year-old round the lawn is going to wear you out.

'Did Mrs Ellis speak to you about the summer holidays, Katie? Before she, er . . .' He trailed off awkwardly beside me.

I nodded. Mrs Ellis had said to me that Brett liked to have the kids more over the summer, when he had more free time. Apparently, I just got paid the same but didn't have to work as much. 'Although I'm sure there's plenty of planning and organizing you can be getting on with,' Mrs E had said, fixing me with those shark-like eyes.

'Season's nearly over,' Brett continued.

'Mmm,' I replied. It's not like I can have a chat with him about how Spartacus have done or anything, after all.

'So, you OK with everything?' Brett said.

Bless him – he's trying to give me less work, whilst paying me the same money and he's checking I'm OK with it. 'Yeah, no, honestly,' I said. 'It's fine. Whatever suits you. I'm happy to cover, whenever you want me to. I mean, not cover – it's my job, isn't it?' Oh shut up, Katie, you're gibbering.

'OK, fine then. I'll let you know dates and times when my schedule's a bit clearer.' And he was off that picnic blanket in a flash. He must seriously wonder about his kids well-being sometimes, knowing that I'm in charge!

The Sunday Newz

Brett 'n' Barcelona Still Hanging in the Balance

It's the final chance for the Spanish hotshots to make the north London club an offer they can't refuse. And let's face it – with the goal-scoring form Brett Ballentine's shown this season, he's definitely worth it.

A club insider said, 'Brett's been playing amazingly recently. He's worth seriously big potatoes to any club.'

Big potatoes? Surely you mean pesetas!

40

Last Friday started out as a pretty normal day. Josh finished work early again and came over to give me a hand with the school run. Then, while I stayed downstairs playing with the kids, he went up to my living room, to try and find a cheap holiday for us on the net, he said.

I was in the middle of a riveting game of Snakes and Ladders in the playroom with the children when Livvy rang me.

'Could we do a swap, Katie?' she asked. 'If I come in early today, could you cover for me later on Thursday?'

'Yeah, sure,' I said, 'suits me fine.' Brilliant, I thought. Livvy coming over straight away meant that I could get on with a romantic evening with Josh.

Livvy said she'd be round in half an hour. When she got to the house we did a quick handover and then I raced upstairs to surprise Josh with the good news.

And surprise him I certainly did.

I opened the door really quietly and tiptoed into my living room. There was Josh sitting at the computer, staring intently at the screen and tapping away at the keys.

I smiled in anticipation of the surprise he was going to get when I snuck up behind him and put my hands over his eyes.

I crept across the room, grinning to myself as his eyes never left the screen. I got right up behind him, raised my hands to his head level and then I spotted it.

Two of Kassie's Armani scarves and a little Louis Vuitton handbag.

And the screen was open at the *IBUY/YOUBUY* website.

My arms dropped by my side. My heart was beating like mad.

'What are you doing, Josh?'

Josh nearly jumped out of his skin. He turned and let out this weird little gasp. And then he started sort of fumbling for the mouse, obviously trying to shut down the screen. But it was way too late for that.

I'd seen enough to know that Josh was selling Kassie's stuff over the Internet.

At that point, all my responses seemed to slow down. I couldn't speak for a moment, and I felt so dizzy, I thought I was going to faint.

But that feeling dissolved, and in its place a sharp bubble of anger rose up. 'How could you do this?' I hissed. I was so incensed I didn't dare move in case I inflicted violence on him. 'Get out! Get out now!'

Josh just swivelled nonchalantly round on his chair, his beautiful face a mask of emotionless calm like he didn't give a damn.

'Oh come on, Katie,' he said, sounding almost bored. 'Chill out. It's not like she's even going to notice.'

I held my hand up to stop him speaking. How could he think, in any way, that what he was doing was OK?

'Why don't you pull up a seat?' Josh said. 'You won't believe what we can get for this stuff . . .'

'We?' I repeated. I looked at him in disbelief. What kind of person did he think I was?

'Calm down, Katie. I know what you earn and I tell you, this is easy money. It's even easier than making a phone call to the showbiz editor at the *Sunday Gossip*—'

'You *what?*' I cut in icily. If my heart had been thudding before, now it was going into overdrive. 'Don't tell me that was *you*, Josh? You leaked the story?'

And just like that, all the strength seemed to leave my body. I backed away towards the sofa and kind of collapsed back on to it.

'Tell me this is a joke, Josh,' I pleaded with my head in my hands. 'You let a sixty-year-old woman get fired because of something *you* did?' I looked up at him, but his expression was impassive.

'Don't come the innocent do-gooder with me, Katie,' Josh said. His eyes seemed so cold now, but they held my gaze. 'What do you care about that tart? And you hated Mrs Ellis – always telling me what a miserable, judgemental old crone she is.'

I shook my head in disbelief. 'It doesn't matter what I said, Josh. I would never have done this to her. Or to Kassie.

Whatever they've done, whoever they are, they don't deserve this. It's sick.'

'What?' Josh sneered. 'Kassie's begging for the publicity. She loves it She's got the morals of an alleycat! You should take a leaf out of her book, if you ask me. Grow a spine while you're at it. Don't you get it? You've got to look after Number One. No one else is going to do it for you, believe me.' He put his hands behind his head, insolently stretching his long legs out in front of him.

I stared at him with utter hatred. 'I thought I told you to leave,' I said evenly. 'I want you to get out right now, before I call the police.'

Josh barked out a nasty laugh. ' Call the police? And what are you going to tell them? "Ooh, officer, I think my boyfriend has been selling my employer's belongings on my computer . . . Honestly, I didn't know anything about it, he just used my password . . ."' He waited, smirking, for the pointlessness of my threat to sink in. It was true, I didn't have a leg to stand on.

Josh got to his feet and picked up his rucksack from the floor, no doubt where he'd dropped it in his eagerness to get on with his dirty work while I'd been distracted downstairs. He slung it over his shoulder and regarded me almost pityingly. 'You know, you're gorgeous, and you're fun to be with, but you're going nowhere. You'll always be just timid little Katie from Hastings.'

It took everything I had not to burst into tears. I could

feel them coming, my eyes were blurring. 'Please go,' I said quietly.

Josh shrugged. He reached out his hand – unbelievably he thought I would take his hand – just as his phone rang. He fished it out of his pocket and answered it.

'Yeah? Hi . . . Hi – I'm on my way now,' he said to whoever it was. 'Yeah, I got let out early in the end . . .' He looked over at me, almost smiling. 'Yeah . . . see you then. Can't wait. Yeah, me too. Love you, Megs.'

And with that he clicked his phone shut and walked out of the door. Out of my life.

I waited precisely five seconds (I know because I counted) before I sank to the floor. I curled up with my arms around myself and cried. And cried. Until darkness engulfed me and I had no more tears left.

41

When I woke up on Saturday morning, it took me a few minutes to register what had happened the night before. I even smiled at the shaft of sunlight coming through the open curtain in my bedroom, and then I thought of getting up to make a cup of tea for myself . . . and for Josh.

Josh. That's when I remembered. I sat up in bed and put my head in my hands. It hadn't been a bad dream; it had actually happened. Josh had really played a blinder this time, and now he was gone. Just like that.

I felt lonelier than I ever had. In the past I'd always had Carly there by my side. My best friend. I could just imagine what she'd say if I phoned her and told her what Josh had done, after I'd virtually accused her of betraying me. She wasn't exactly going to be sympathetic. And if she told me where to go I wouldn't blame her. But I had to try and build bridges – she was all I had left. I'd been an idiot and I needed her.

I took a long bath, dressed and forced down a cup of tea, though I couldn't eat a thing. Then I sat on the sofa just holding my phone for ages, scrolling up and down my contacts. I would get to Carly's number and nearly select Call, only to chicken out. In the end, I did it, but my hands were shaking.

'Carly?'

I could almost feel the tension in the pause before she answered. And when she did she sounded weary.

'What do you want?'

'Carly, I know you're really angry with me. I've been so stupid, really out of order – I realize that. You've always been there for me, always been straight with me, and I made a huge mistake.'

There was silence.

'I've split up with Josh.' I tried to keep my voice flat but I couldn't help the wobble in the last word.

'Right,' Carly said. 'Is that what this is all about? You've split up with Mr Wonderful and now I'm expected to be a shoulder to cry on?'

I wasn't going to lie about it. 'It's not that . . . well, in a way, yes – it's made me realize who my true friends are. I've been a fool, trusting Josh over you. I should have listened to you. I should have listened to everyone who told me . . . But this job, Carly, being here . . . It's been so hard . . .' I couldn't help myself, tears were coming thick and fast now. I tried to go on, to tell her what had happened, but my throat felt constricted. I was literally choked up.

If I had been expecting Carly to suddenly melt and forgive me, though, I was wrong.

'Yeah, whatever.' Carly sounded hard. 'I'm not sure

it *is* just the job, Katie. Perhaps you've always been selfish and it's just brought out the worst in you. Anyway . . .' She paused and I heard the front door slamming. 'I can't talk about this now. Gemma's just got in from her night shift and I need to see her. I'm sorry about you and Josh, but I'm not ready to forgive you – not yet. Maybe not ever.'

I let out the breath I had been holding in, feeling that the world was collapsing around me.

'Bye, Katie. Maybe see you around,' Carly said softly, and she hung up.

The last two weeks since that phone call I've just about managed to drag myself through the days. The first time I split up with Josh was different: I had dreams, I still loved him, I ate myself up with jealousy over Megan. But this time it isn't like that. I feel nothing for him. And before I had my best friend there, ready to joke me out of my blues, give me a hug when I hit a low point. Now there is nobody.

I thought about going home last weekend, but I couldn't even bring myself to do that. I've told Mum about splitting up with Josh – not all the details; I'm ashamed enough without opening that particular can of worms – and she tried really hard to keep the 'I told you so' out of her voice.

'Oh, love, I'm so sorry. Why don't you come home, sweetheart, let your old mum look after you?'

I sniffed. Mum being kind induced the by-now-familiar waterworks.

'Thanks, Mum. I'm OK. I'll *be* OK, anyway, but I'm

needed here with the kids. Kassie's got all this stuff on at the moment . . .' My words trailed off half-heartedly. Much as the thought of home and a hug from my mum was all I wanted, I couldn't run the risk of bumping into Josh, or any of my friends. I'd be a laughing stock. And I needed to show Mum that I was a big girl now. Not the loser little kid I felt inside.

'So I won't be home for a bit. I'll be fine, I've always got—'

'Yes, at least you've got Carly there, eh?' Mum cut in, trying to be reassuring. If only she knew.

'Yeah, well . . . gotta go,' I lied. 'I've left the bath running.'

Close-up 2006

Celebland – fill in the blanks!

Kassie Ballentine

People are always surprised when I . . . Say I don't really understand football!
If I wasn't a celebrity I'd be . . . A banker – might as well count other people's money!
My favourite drink in the morning is . . . Black coffee. It keeps me perky for the rest of the day.
I feel most comfortable when I'm . . . Slouching around in the playroom with my lovely children.

A perfect night would be . . . Snuggled up on the sofa with Brett and the kids.

When I look in the mirror I see . . . Someone who's trying to be a good person.

I'm in a bad mood when . . . Someone disses me who's never even met me.

The sexiest smell is . . . Sunday dinner!

My weirdest dream was about . . . Having a big row with Arsène Wenger. Never gonna happen. What was that all about?

When I'm hungry I eat . . . Loads! I'm not discerning. I'll just grab whatever's in the fridge – or the cookie jar!

I'm scared of . . . Spiders. Brett has to get them out of the room. I turn into a really screamy girl.

My earliest memory is . . . Playing with next-door's rabbit.

What I liked most about school was . . . Leaving it!

42

I'm feeling a bit better. I've been keeping myself really busy, looking after the kids, helping Kassie organize her charity ball. I never thought I'd say this but she's been a godsend – I've actually found her constant wittering on about herself a pleasant distraction from my own thoughts. And she seemed to sense I was a bit down – she'd certainly noticed that Josh hadn't been around lately. In the end I had to tell her we'd split up. Obviously I kept the catalyst for our break-up well and truly hidden. Instead I used Megan as the excuse.

When I'd finished telling her, Kassie let out this big, worldly-wise sigh, and gave my shoulder a little squeeze. I think she was enjoying being the confidante for a change.

'Oh well, sweetheart, sounds like you're well rid there. Shame, because he seemed like such a nice boy. But you're young, you'll find someone else in no time.' She paused, looking thoughtful for a second or two. 'Actually, Ken's got a younger brother you might go for. Well, he's a bit older than you – about ten years older, I think – but he's loaded, and not that bad-looking. He's just split up with Miranda Miskin – you know, the Page Three model . . . ?'

213

'Er, thanks, Kassie,' I said, horrified but trying not to show it. 'I don't think I'm quite ready to get back on the horse yet. I'm going to give the single life a go for now.'

I almost smiled to myself then. A few weeks before I would have been rushing to relay the whole conversation to Carly, and the two of us would have been in stitches over Creepy Ken's little brother. Imagine being in any way involved with that man's family. Ugh!

Talking of Carly, there has been some progress there. I tried phoning her again, and repeating how very sorry I was, how I would do anything to get our friendship back on track, and please could she give me another chance. I told her the full story of Josh, didn't spare any of the details. And this time, I sensed Carly was softening. Halfway through the phone call, I had another blub, which turned into a full-on hiccup-inducing breakdown, and she kind of had no choice but to realize that I was properly in a bad way and genuinely sorry.

'Listen, Katie,' she said, almost gently. 'I don't know if things can go back to how they were between us. But I still care about you.' She sighed. 'If you want to meet for a coffee or something, that might be OK. I can't promise we're going to be best buddies again, but I don't like hearing you so upset. Honestly, if I get my hands on that git, I am going to rip his head off,' she added, and just for a minute, the old, loyal Carly was back. It gave me a bit of hope, anyway.

So tonight we're having our first post-traumatic get-together. We were meant to be going out to eat – just to

Wagamamas for noodles – but I've had to cry off (eating that is) as I've spent the whole day stuffing food down my mooey.

I met Carly for a drink instead.

It started off a bit awkwardly. I can't say I blame her, but I decided to give it time.

'I really am sorry, you know, Carly,' I said.

'Yeah, I know,' she shrugged. 'Listen, Katie. I possibly was a bit hard on you. Knowing what's been going on, I can see why you might be constantly paranoid. I'm just glad my life is so normal, to be honest. Boring in many ways, I know, but at least I don't have to do all that pretending. Poor old Mrs Ellis, eh?' She smiled naughtily. 'Never did warm to the old bat, but she didn't deserve that!'

I nodded and looked around cautiously. 'I sent an anonymous letter to the *Sunday Gossip* saying she's innocent,' I whispered.

Carly looked at me aghast for a minute, then her face lit up in one enormous smile. 'Way to go, Katie Meredith. Now that's the Katie I know and love . . .' I kind of knew then that it was going to be OK with Carls.

'I wonder if they'll print it?' she said, more to herself than to me. Then silence again. Just as I was starting to feel relaxed – and so relieved – Carly let me know she wasn't going to let me off scot-free. She swirled her drink in her glass and fixed me with a steely look.

'Look, it's over, Katie,' she said. 'What's done is done. But I tell you, you'd better remember who your friends are in future. Because if you stick around with the Ballentines, there's going to be more of this ahead, you know.'

I nodded silently. I knew she was right, and it wasn't a thought I felt too comfortable with.

'So, you going to have anything?' She indicated the bar menu.

'Hmm,' I said, patting my stomach. 'Honestly, you won't believe how much I've eaten today – Kassie's had the caterers round so that she can sample the food for her big charity ball. But she doesn't actually eat, as you know, so muggins here was given that particular task. Needless to say, if I never see a salmon filo pastry parcel again, it'll be a day too soon!'

'Poor baby,' Carly said mock sympathetically. 'The terrible things they put you through in that house . . .'

Running around doing chores in aid of the ball – the very mention of which now sends me into a coma of boredom – is what I've been spending pretty much all of my sad single life doing since then. I've probably only had sole care of the kids for a couple of days a week. The rest of the time I'm like Kassie's monkey, which keeps me nice and distracted, I admit. Kassie's got herself a PA who does all the big stuff, but for all the little bits and bobs, I'm Kassie's yes girl.

'Do you like this one, Katie?'

'Yes, Kassie.'

'I think these napkins, don't you?'

'Yes, Kassie.'

'The purple or the pink?'

'Pur—'

'Pink, I think.'

'Mmm, me too!'

Sunday Gossip

Mrs E Is Innocent

A mystery source has revealed to us that Enid Ellis, ex-housekeeper to Kassie and Brett Ballentine, is in fact not the perpetrator of the story leaked exclusively to the *Sunday Gossip* of Kassie's faked miscarriage. The source, who wouldn't reveal their identity, said that they were responsible . . . ! OK, if that's what you want us to believe, we'll start printing the 'Mrs E Is Innocent' posters pronto!

43

The big night has finally arrived! And though I hate to admit it I am actually a bit excited. Maybe that's because I've got diddly-squat else in my life to look forward to, but still. Kassie might be mad as a nut a lot of the time, but it looks like her psychotic-lunatic-on-speed approach has actually paid off this time! I mean, everything seems to be in place for one heck of an event.

She is the absolute Queen of Kitsch and I think, for once, her lack of taste has actually become an asset. It's like she's recognized it and exploited it and has turned her crass style into the new cool. And Richmond Park is definitely the place to be tonight. The woman hasn't just got your usual D and C listers – she's actually managed to pull in your As and Bs as well! I think the amount of coverage she's got herself and her charity has meant that anyone who doesn't want to be seen ignoring the plight of poor suffering sick people had better put in an appearance.

Yep, maybe Kassie has finally found her niche. Big Party Organizer Supremo. All this time she's been trying to prove to everyone that she's a somebody, and in her desperation she's usually muffed it. But this time, the project was made for her. She's like a little despot in Armani jeans – if she wants something done, it gets done, or heads roll. I still kind of admire her. She doesn't care about her background, she isn't afraid of anybody. As far as she's concerned, no one is better than her, and if they think they are they'd better watch out!

I'm feeling bad about everything that's happened though, so I'm determined not to put a foot wrong from now on. And I heard Kassie talking to Creepy Ken on the phone this morning. Apparently Mrs E has got a job presenting a telly programme about how to run your household with celebrity style. I don't think Kassie's best pleased, but what can she do?

She is on manic hyper-drive today – earpiece clamped on so tightly I think it might have to be surgically removed – along with the clipboard that might have to be prised out of her hand before the evening's over.

Brett has taken Regan and Maxi out – both Kassie and I put up a lame protest but actually I think we were both quite glad. I'm so excited about tonight; it's the first time I've felt sort of good about anything since all the hideousness with Josh. I don't know if my nannying skills would have been quite up to par! Goodness knows, they've been a bit ropey for the past couple of weeks anyway. Plus there's a whole afternoon of beautifying to be had – and I couldn't possibly be expected to miss out on that now, could I?

Brett is under threat of death if he doesn't bring the kids

back on time. He seems kind of subdued and distracted, to be honest. But then I guess it's so not his moment to shine, and with Kassie definitely grabbing all the glory maybe he's feeling a bit left out . . .

Anyway, we've got last-minute details to sort out this morning. I've got a list of suppliers to chase to make sure everything's where it should be and on schedule too. And then it's facials, hair, make-up, frocks, etc. Then I've got to get the kids ready as they are going to come along for the early part of the evening – there's a funfair being constructed just for the event. Not a scuzzy town-green one with dodgy lads and even dodgier rides, but this really old-fashioned affair – all twinkly lights, carousels, coconut shies and even a tunnel of love! And all the people running the stalls are done up in Victorian costume so it's kind of authentic and very atmospheric. I'm sure Regan and Maxi will love it.

Then I'm going to bring them back home, hand them over to Livvy, who's going to have the onerous task of bringing them back down to earth and getting them into bed even though there'll probably be half a ton of sugar in the form of candyfloss coursing through their veins – so not my problem – and I'm going back to the ball! Hurrah!

What a night. I don't even know where to start. At the beginning of the evening I was just a bag of nerves, but kind of nice excited nerves. But now, well – I'm just blown away by what's happened. I mean, I'm still a bag of nerves, but these are different, not-nice nerves – like I'm standing on the edge of a cliff. More on that later; first I'd better backtrack a bit.

Obviously you know what the day was like, manic phone calls in between manic pampering (if there can be such a thing). Kassie swinging from evil witch to meine hostess taking good-luck phone calls with all the grace a magnanimous benefactor such as herself could muster. It really was her Cinderella moment and she was going to milk it for all it was worth.

The kids got back in the middle of the afternoon and I whisked them off for a bath and a spruce-up. I'd already told them that they weren't to put their clothes on until the very last minute – one speck of dirt and I was a dead woman.

They were obviously excited too. It wasn't like they really knew what was going on, but they could tell from the way the grown-ups were all in a tizz that something was going down.

Kassie had got them these ridiculous Victorian outfits – kind of Little Lord Fauntleroy. But I have to admit they did actually look quite cute. Although I think Regan was mortified to be wearing a full-length frilly frock. But once we got there, all thoughts of what they were wearing flew from their heads. The funfair was like every child's dream!

I had chosen a fantastic D&G dress, courtesy of Kassie. Kind of like a silvery sheath with all this diamante detail – just incredible. It had built-in corsetry so there were no bumps where there shouldn't be, and I have to admit I felt like a million dollars. The fabric was all silky and swishy and made a kind of quiet whooshing noise every time I moved. My hair had been swept up into this amazing chignon, really smooth and sophisticated, scraped back at the front with the straightest parting you've ever seen in your life and then curled into this kind of reef knot in the nape of my neck (I am so glad I've spent the last year growing out my Amélie-bob). I've no idea how the stylist did it, but it looked fabulous. The only drawback was that I was absolutely banned from in any way touching my hair for the rest of the night. Apparently even a smoothing pat and the whole thing would be ruined! Fortunately for me Kassie was having stylists and make-up artists in situ to make sure everyone was at their touched-up best for the exclusive photographs. Reckon I'll be at the front of the queue for that. Oh my God, I think my sudden wannabe celebrity status is definitely going to my head!

Like I said, the kids were only to be there for the early part of the evening and then I was to take them home. But they absolutely loved going on all the rides and eating their own bodyweight in toffee apples and candyfloss! At one point, after a particularly enthusiastic spin on the old-fashioned waltzer, I thought Maxi might be about to lose his lunch. But a little quiet sit-down and a few deep breaths and he was well up for a load more rubbish to eat and several more goes on any of the rides he was big enough for – which, as we were talking Victoriana rather than high-tech terror rides, was most of them.

But of course as soon as the celebs started arriving Kassie whisked the children into the enormous marquee to be part of the photo-shoot extravaganza being unleashed. I don't think I've ever seen so many flashbulbs going off in my whole life. I've been to a few dos now as you know, but this was like *the* event of the year.

For all that Kassie has a love/hate relationship with the media, she knows how to work it when it counts. Flirting with the paparazzi, flashing a bit of leg, bending over in a Marilyn Monroe-esque pout. Gathering the children into her like she's the yummy mummy of the century and then – as soon as the crowds had moved on and her guests were safely in the marquee with the official *OK* exclusive photographer – she brought them right back over to me.

'OK, kids, time to go home.' And I'll tell you what, there was absolutely no arguing with her. Within about ten minutes of Kassie's decree, myself and both children were in the car and heading back to Knightsbridge. I did think we might get a bit of a paddy out of one (or both) of them, but to be honest, I think they knew it wouldn't get them anywhere, so they just didn't bother.

'Did you have a nice time?' I asked as we whisked through the summer evening streets.

'Yeah, it was wicked,' Regan smiled.

'Yeah,' Maxi copied. 'Wicked!'

'What was the best bit?' I asked.

'Going on the waltzer and Maxi nearly being sick!' Regan laughed.

'I wasn't sick, Katie, was I?' Maxi wailed.

'No, darling, you were fine,' I soothed, stroking his moist hair. They were both a bit hot and sticky from an evening spent stuck in restrictive outfits.

'Once when we went to the funfair with Daddy—' Maxi stopped himself in mid-sentence. 'We didn't say goodbye to Daddy!' He sounded genuinely concerned.

'Don't worry,' I said. 'I'm sure Daddy will understand. Besides, I expect he was busy helping Mummy entertain all their guests.'

Maxi looked unsure.

'I didn't see Daddy for ages,' Regan said. 'Was he still there?'

'Yes, I'm sure he was,' I said vaguely. 'And I'm sure he'll give you a kiss when he gets home and make sure you're all tucked up in bed.'

The kids smiled as I gazed out of the car window. London looked like it was wilting in the summer heat. I stifled a yawn, suddenly feeling quite tired. My mind drifted. Come to think of it, I hadn't seen Brett for quite some time either.

Getting the kids to bed wasn't that bad after all. Livvy and I kind of did it together: she took charge of Regan and I looked after Maxi. Once they'd told Livvy all about everything they'd done and how exciting it all was – and I'd told her about all the celebs that had been there and what they'd been wearing – they were quite happy to settle into their normal evening routine.

It was only at the final point that there was a minor crisis – which turned into a major crisis for me.

The thing was, Maxi has a favourite toy – Billy Bear – and there is no sleeping without it being in the bed. The problem is that Billy Bear gets dragged around everywhere that Maxi goes, and Maxi not being the most observant of four-year-olds is in the habit of putting Billy Bear down to focus on something else and then forgetting about the poor fat fellow all together . . . until bedtime, when it's total crisis meltdown if that bear is not found and put in bed with him.

When Maxi first announced that Billy Bear was missing, I did have a slight panic on myself. One – the bear could be anywhere and, horror of horrors, I couldn't even be sure he hadn't taken it to the ball with him. And two – I wanted to get back to the ball, not to find the bear, but to continue my celeb-spotting and do a bit of serious gawping! I wasn't sure my conscience would let me go gallivanting if I had to leave Maxi in a state of genuine heartbreak.

Livvy and I started desperately trying to get Maxi to remember when he'd last had Billy Bear. Not an easy thing to try and get an overwrought four-year-old to do.

'Did you have him in the car?'

'Nooooo, I want my Billy Bear!'

'Did you have him in the garden earlier?'

'I don't knooooooooow . . .'

'You had him when you went to see Daddy,' Regan interrupted helpfully.

'Where was that then?' I asked, desperate to give my head a good scratch but aware that my carefully coiffed hair wouldn't take it.

Maxi just wailed again while Regan said, 'Um, I think he went to see him when he was doing letters and things . . .'

'So was he in the office?' I asked.

'I think so,' Regan said.

Livvy started getting to her feet. 'Don't worry,' I said, virtually leaping up, 'I'll go.' The sooner I got the stuffed creature, the sooner I was back in la-la land surrounded by delicious nibbles and free-flowing champagne. I don't think anyone in a D&G dress has ever moved so fast.

But I tell you, had I known what else I'd find in Brett's office, I might have been a bit less keen.

Close-up 2005

I'M A RELUCTANT WAG!

Although Kassie Ballentine likes to play down her WAG status, she admits she has tons of designer handbags – bought with her own money, she's quick to add – and she's proud of her handmade £7,000 Jimmy Choos, a gift from the designer himself.

44

Dear Kassie

This is probably the hardest letter I am ever going to have to write. I truly, truly don't want to cause you hurt or pain, but I don't love you. And I think if you are really honest with yourself you don't love me either. I pretty much accept the fact that you used me as a stepping stone to get what you want out of life – money and celebrity – and I don't feel bitter: we all do what we can to get by and you've given me the most important things I could ever have, my children.

I am going to accept the transfer offer to Barcelona and, I might as well tell you now as I'm sure you'll hear about it soon enough, I will be going there with Beth and my son, Sam. I have only recently found out that Beth was pregnant when you and I got together. Let's face it – as far as I was concerned you were only ever meant to be a one-night stand. I felt so ashamed of myself for cheating on Beth and then, of course, you told me you were pregnant and Beth didn't want anything more to do with me and the rest is history.

But things have changed. I have been seeing a lot of Beth again and we both realize that our feelings for each other are as strong as they ever were, and that it is time to put the past behind us and start again.

I love her, I always have, and she loves me. Although I've tried to fight it for the sake of our children, I can't live this lie any more. I need to be with Beth and our son. I will not fight you for money, I will give you a very generous settlement. But I will fight you for custody as I feel the children will have a happier and more stable home with me and Beth and their brother Sam. However, I am prepared to let them see you as much as you, and they, would like. Give it some thought, Kass – don't just go off on one. Try, for once, to put your children first.

Yours

Brett

Talk about a total heart-stopping moment.

It was so ironic. Resting right on top of that letter was Billy Bear. I mean, right on top of it! It kind of made me feel sick. Imagine if Maxi could read! It just didn't bear thinking about.

I'd rushed into the office, seen Billy lying there large as life and snatched him off the desk whilst whisking round to head for the door. In my hurry, I'd wafted the letter off the desk and on to the floor. So I turned around, snatched it up and went to lay it back down on the desk. And then my eye just caught on the first line and well . . . I honestly hadn't meant to read it. I put it down like I wasn't going to, but it was kind of magnetic. I mean, you'd have to be super-human not to, wouldn't you?

Anyway, I did read it, and once I'd read it there was no unreading it. Maxi and Regan's little lives were about to be

228

shattered and, so far, I was the only person apart from their father and Beth who knew it.

I thought about Kassie. I suppose her life would be shattered too. But I couldn't help feeling that she'd probably use it to her advantage. What is it they say? No publicity's bad publicity.

I sat down in Brett's swivel chair and, completely forgetting all hair-styling instructions, held my head in my hands and stared at the letter. I really did feel sick. How could I go back to those little children and act like nothing had happened?

I cuddled Billy Bear to me and pressed my nose against his soft, patchy, well-worn fur. He smelled like Maxi. Like childhood, all safe and snuggly.

Perhaps I could find Brett at the ball, try to reason with him. Perhaps if he knew how much it would hurt the children he'd change his mind? Surely they were worth more than his childhood romance and the son he'd never even known? I knew what betrayal felt like, and I wouldn't wish it on anyone.

I don't even know how I made it back to the children's room without heaving. And it didn't help matters to see how happy Maxi was to have Billy Bear returned to him. His little tear-stained face just lit up and he buried it into Billy's tummy. 'Oh, Billy, you are so naughty,' his little muffled voice seeped through, 'but I'm so glad Katie found you.' He re-emerged from his snuggle and gave me a ferocious cuddle.

I could feel my eyes welling up. Livvy noticed and gave me a quizzical look, but I guess she just thought I was a bit drunk and soppy.

I cleared my throat. 'I better get back to the ball. Mummy will be wondering where I've got to.' I crouched down to give the kids another cuddle, squished between their little bodies. I'd do anything to keep them from harm, I really would, but I was beginning to realize that there were some things in this life that were quite simply beyond my control.

'Now, be good for Livvy and I'll come in to check on you later. Night night.' I gave them both a kiss.

'Night night, Katie,' they chorused.

'Love you,' said Maxi.

'Yeah, love you,' said Regan.

That lump in my throat was getting dangerously uncomfortable. I gulped and took a deep breath. 'I love you too.'

I may not be able to keep these kids totally safe, I know that, but I'm damned if anyone's going to stop me from trying. As I walked out of that house, I had a new steely determination. Brett Ballentine may well be the biggest thing in the known universe and I may well be the little man on the totem pole, but I tell you, big-shot or not, he was certainly going to get a piece of my mind. This year had been one screw-up, lie and bit of treachery after another – perhaps I could finally get something right.

I started looking for Brett as soon as I arrived back at the venue. If I hesitated at all, I didn't think I would go through with it. Kassie, of course, was completely oblivious – she hadn't seen him for hours and frankly she really wasn't bothered. I had to sort of remind myself that it wasn't her I was doing this for – it was Maxi and Regan. I could understand Brett's reservations about Kassie, but the children . . . And he had *married* her. Didn't that count for anything these days?

Brett was harder to find than a needle in a haystack. It probably didn't help that I didn't know that many people or, more to the point, they didn't know me, so it wasn't like I could go around asking all and sundry if they'd seen him. I mean, we're talking about Mr Mega-pants here – people are very protective of him, even if they don't even know him themselves. It's comical really, when you consider I've shared a picnic blanket with him and partaken in quite a few rounds of hide-and-seek. Let's face it, with the sort of inside knowledge I'd got lately, I think I could pretty confidently say I know him better than most people.

Anyway, in the end I had to resort to asking Creepy Ken. In retrospect, probably a bad move. I don't trust that guy: I think he's a totally backstabbing you-know-what. He's definitely in the no-publicity-is-bad-publicity school of thought – no matter who gets hurt in the media fallout.

I tried my best to act like it was no big deal.

'Have you seen Brett anywhere?' I asked, casually.

I could see his little antennae twitching instantly. 'No, baby, why?'

'Oh, I just wanted to ask him something.'

'Something that can't wait, eh?'

I smiled through gritted teeth. 'It's just about Maxi's teddy. We couldn't find it and he really can't sleep without it. I just thought Brett might have an idea where it is.'

'Now you mention it, I haven't seen him around all evening.' Creepy Ken's head swivelled, his beady eyes leering. 'I wonder where he can be?'

Ugh! He really is like a slug in a suit, that guy.

'Don't worry about it,' I said quickly. 'Livvy's probably found it by now anyway.'

'Well, baby,' he sneered, 'if I see Brett, I'll be sure to pass that vital message on.'

God, what a git. I can't believe he ever was a child – I think he just emerged as a fully formed evil adult out of some alien pod.

I pushed my way through the hordes in the marquee. Kassie was holding court, but managed to grab my arm as I passed by.

'Party bags at midnight, Katie. I want you to help me give them out.'

Obviously Kassie wasn't giving them all out – she had some hired help to do that. But she had a few exclusive numbers for people she particularly thought might be able to give her career a bit of a boost. Shameless, I tell you.

'Have you seen that idiot husband of mine?' Kassie

slurred slightly. 'I'd better get one picture of the two of us together, put paid to any of these bloody marriage-on-the-rocks rumours, eh?' She cackled to herself. 'Haven't seen the big drip all bloody night; probably sulking, bless him.'

Kassie almost made me lose my resolve. She didn't deserve Brett, but it wasn't fair that she didn't know what was going on right under her very nose.

Where *was* Brett? A wave of panic washed over me again. God, what if he'd already gone? Done a flit? It's not like Kassie would notice. I mean, she didn't pay any attention to him at the best of times, but the ball would be the perfect cover.

I ran out of the marquee. It was about half past nine by now and the light was fading fast. The fairground was still going strong. I raced past all the rides and stands, the sounds and smells assaulting my senses as I tried to pick out Brett in the milling crowds. It was hopeless. How the hell could I hope to find him, let alone have a quiet word in his ear, with all this going on?

And then I had an idea – call it a hunch. I ran to the cloakroom and took my coat and then headed outside to the exit, to the street and a waiting cab. Something told me I needed to get home, back to the Ballentines'. I told the driver to go as fast as he could. Time seemed very much of the essence.

I told the cab to stop at the top of the street, and I quickly crept the rest of the way. Using my security key, I slipped through the gates and headed for the little copse of trees by the side entrance – it was the way I usually entered the house. I was almost out of breath and paused a moment when I reached the first tree, leaning against it and feeling the rough coolness of the bark on my forehead. It was weirdly soothing.

The night air was still quite warm with leftover heat from the day, and I started feeling a bit doubtful about my plan. What did I think I was going to do anyway? Like it was any of my business. Did I imagine it was going to be a case of 'Katie saves the day' and everyone lives happily ever after?

It was then that I heard voices coming from the other side of the trees – nearer to the road. I crept back the way I had come, and stopped behind an enormous bush.

One of the voices had a soft, feminine, northern lilt and the other one was unmistakably Brett Ballentine.

My heart leapt in my chest. My little peace-making expedition was all very well in theory, but now it came to the grim reality I wasn't sure I could go through with it.

But then I thought of the kids and how devastated they'd be if Brett and Kassie split up. Perfect parents they certainly ain't, but family's family, right? I took a dangerous peek around the foliage. Brett and Beth were standing in full view of the road with their arms around each other. I guess they must have planned this little rendezvous, knowing that everyone and his wife would be at Kassie's event. And I would have spoken to them. I swear I would. But . . .

'I'm crazy about you.'

At first I smirked. Come on, Brett, can't you come up with anything better than that?

'I'm so sorry about . . . about everything . . .'

'Ssshhh, it's OK . . .'

They were kind of leaning into each other and she was stroking his hair. I just didn't have the nerve to walk in on that scene, not just yet.

'I messed up.' Brett went on. 'But from now on, things are going to be different. I'm going to make up for everything.' He sounded like he was crying. 'I just can't be without you any more, B. I've really tried with Kassie, but she's never, ever going to make me happy. Not like *we* were happy . . . You've always been the one. You were all I ever wanted and when I think how I screwed it all up . . .'

She just kept saying, 'Shhh' and stroking his hair. It felt all wrong that I was there. It was such a private moment and there was I, earwigging. Story of my life. 'We're going to be a proper family now. You and all my beautiful kids.'

If this were a scene from a romcom, and I was watching it on DVD with Carly, we'd both have been blubbing over our Häagen Dazs by now. Beth was snivelling and sobbing and Brett was snivelling and sobbing too. I'll be honest, I never thought he had it in him to be so, well, soppy.

Brett's absolutely right, I thought. He and Kassie are a match made in hell. It's obvious – they bring out the worst in each other. I looked up at the clear midnight sky, searching for stars, and I could feel those tears pricking my eyes again. Sometimes you have to seize happiness when it comes. If you let it slip away, you'll always wonder what might have been. Even Josh, I thought, with a stab of hurt, even giving Josh a second chance. If I hadn't, I would always have wondered, did I make a mistake in not taking him back? At least I did it, and I found out that he is not the one, *definitely* not the one for me. Now I can move on. No regrets.

The kids will survive this, I thought. And I turned to sneak back inside, leaving the lovebirds to make their plans.

But as I quietly climbed the steps to the side door, I felt a movement to my left. I turned, and there, standing in the road, only yards from Brett and Beth, was a girl. She looked about my age – dark-haired, pretty – and she was holding a serious-looking camera in her hand. Before I could register what was going on, there was the snap of a twig and then a flash. I stood frozen, unable to move, and she and I locked gazes. The look on her face was determined, resolute and satisfied. Not satisfied in the way that a pap looks when he takes a picture. It was something else, something more considered, more sensitive maybe . . .

I hesitated only a second before I dashed inside as softly as I could. I wouldn't be in long, just enough time to pack my bags and leave a note. I love Maxi and Regan, truly I do, but I'd had enough. I was going home. I'd find a nice normal nannying job, and try and get my nice normal life back once again.

I didn't even think about the girl with the camera. Whoever she was, good luck to her. I had a feeling she was going to need it.

Turn over to read the

consequence

of this story...

consequences...
The camera never lies

1

When I was little, I used to lie in bed with the curtains open, my eyes fixed on the bright, orange glow of the street lamp right outside my window, outside the cosy, warm world my mum and dad had created for me. It wasn't the noise of the cars driving past that I was interested in, or the voices of people coming into the other terraced houses on my street; just the light and the black sky beyond it. I wanted to dive out of my bedroom window into the darkness beyond the light and see what the world had to offer me.

It was beautiful and it was frightening at the same time.

And I dreamed of my future, and what my life would be like past the safety of the cosy orange light.

Then one Christmas, when I was about seven, Dad gave me a little camera, one of those point and click ones with the pop-up flash, because I had been going on at him for months about taking pictures like I had seen him do so many times on holidays. I think he only did it to shut me up. I was a talkative girl. That hasn't changed. And all I ever talked about was the way things looked, how this should be changed to match that, what went with what, how this looked better here. I loved to get everything looking just right.

Once all the excitement of Christmas had died down, I finally found the courage to take my first ever picture. I didn't want to waste that moment by rushing it. Somehow I knew it was way too important.

I was in bed in the dark, with the curtains open as usual, and suddenly flakes of grey began to flicker and dive around the bright lamp in the street outside. Quickly the snow swirled and darted, like it was burning in the flame of my light. The sky was heavy and the street silent, as the snow crept into the gaps and corners, filling them with white.

I took a beautiful picture that night, my first ever. The red button for the flash came on and I pressed myself against the cold window, training the auto focus lens on the snowy scene. Before I even looked through the viewfinder or clicked the shutter, I could already see the photograph in my mind, framed and perfectly formed, and when I was finished I didn't need to look again at the world outside the window. I knew I'd captured it just right.

Of course, two weeks later the photo came out as a splodgy brown mess. There were no snowflakes, no magical light, no brooding sky. In fact, nobody could tell what the picture was meant to show, except me. But still, I'd seen the picture in my head so clearly, and now all I needed to do was find out how to make it come to life using the camera.

I was hooked.

* * *

Now, years later, and two days after I took the picture that changed my life, I held on to the photo, kept it in my darkroom at home, refused to even touch it. It stayed on the drying line, facing the wall, away from any prying parental eyes. They never went in there anyway, and I always made sure I kept it locked, especially when I'd done a few shots they wouldn't have approved of, and I didn't want to take the risk. I didn't know what I was going to do. I was a bit shocked by what I'd photographed and a bit stunned by what I could do with it.

I went to college and did my A level coursework; ignoring the idiot boys who tried to wind me up on the bus home; chatting to people on MSN and my mobile and trying to avoid chocolate and my mum's baking.

Everything was so normal on the surface: I was Natalie. That much was the same: a bit weird, a bit quirky, depending on who you talked to. I wasn't the most popular girl at college, but then I wasn't an outcast. I had a couple of close friends who I chatted with on MSN about my 'secret'. One of them was Ravi, whose greatest ambition was to be on *Big Brother* and be the first gay Asian teenage cross-dresser to win it. Every year he got more hopeful when that series' gay cross-dresser was evicted early on.

RaviBUFF: Look Nat, you have to go for it. What's the problem? These people are publicity addicts anyway.

IMAGEGrrl: Yeah that's true.

RaviBUFF: They spend their whole lives going

after it. You would just be giving them some more. I should know darling. I'm dying for some xx.

IMAGEGrrl: You're a sad ass Rav. It's not like you ever go out in your dresses anyway. What if they get their bodyguards to come after me? Will you save me?

RaviBUFF: As if. Seriously, though. I'll do it for you if you haven't got the balls?

IMAGEGrrl: Listen, I'm the only one with the balls in this relationship Rav, and don't forget it!

RaviBUFF: OK, point taken, but even more reason you should go for it. Evie thinks so too.

IMAGEGrrl: I know, she told me. She did make me think.

Evie was the third part of our little triangle. She was like a more reliable, more sensible version of me. If even *she* thought I should sell the picture, then maybe I wasn't going to be sent to hell and eternal damnation after all.

There were times during those two days when I made myself forget about the picture that had burned itself into my mind from the moment I had taken it. But how different could things get? Surely it was only a bunch of pixels on special paper?

Deep down, of course, I knew better. It was an unexploded bomb.

And I knew I had to make a decision. Me. Nobody else.

Clive, my long-suffering Media teacher at college, was

always going on at me about pursuing proper photography. Clive was a photographer too; part time when he wasn't teaching, and he was pretty good in a 'local scenery and fairly-interesting-still-life' kind of way. He was talking about 'integrity in art' – making sure I knew how much store he set by serious, rather than frivolous, focus in a chosen craft.

'Natalie, you have to make sure you stay true to your talent, work for it, squeeze every ounce of life out of it. Never ever let yourself down by selling out for the money. There are artists and there are salesmen. You are an artist! Don't let your talent be used for anything other than art, OK? NO wedding photographs!'

I knew his heart was in the right place, but sometimes I couldn't see the difference. Tracey Emin made great art and Annie Leibovich (my hero!) took amazing pictures, but I couldn't say that what Tracey Emin did was exactly 'serious' – even if she thought so. Their pictures always looked like they'd had fun working, despite them being 'high art', as everyone said. I didn't see why you always had to suffer for your craft. What was wrong with enjoying it, too?

I would sit down hugging a mug of coffee in the photo lab at college during break and try to reassure Clive about my 'seriousness'.

'I know what you're saying, Clive, I really do, and I'll do my best, I promise.' I pretended to hide in shame the David Beckham pencil case I'd had since I was fourteen, which I now used as an ironic comment on media manipulation of young teens. 'And when I'm really famous and rich I'll make

243

sure I tell everyone who'll listen that it was you who inspired me to put the art in my photographs. Especially if I get more money for saying so.'

Clive winced and took a swig from his cup and I smiled. He looked like some old photographer from the 1960s, all long grey hair and wrinkled face. He probably didn't have a lot of money, and he'd never made his mark, artistically speaking. But he was kind and meant well.

'Do you remember what you said about that picture of the swans that I did for my Art GCSE? That it belonged on a birthday card from Clinton Cards?'

Clive twitched a hairy eyebrow in my general direction and sighed heavily.

'Now that, Natalie de Silva, was a complete travesty. You should have been shot for that. All function and no form. I'm only grateful that you've taken the right path since then and listened to me. Your photographs betray talent indeed. I hope that one day you will be coming back to see me with a magnificent portfolio, and the respect of your fellow artists. That's what you need to aspire to in our profession, believe me.'

The thing is, I did believe him in some ways. Sure, I wanted to be an acclaimed artist, get featured in the *Sunday Times* magazine for my revolutionary pictures of rock stars in their underpants, or for revealing the suffering of an undiscovered Amazonian tribe or images of war that defined a generation. I could even see myself photographing the new Marilyn Monroe in her early years, taking the picture that catapulted her to greatness.

It was just that I also wanted fame; I wanted to have the global masses look at what I'd done and know my name. Was that too much to ask?

Most photographers had to make do with a little gallery in a back street in London showing ten of their pictures to three people a day, if they were lucky. But they usually had a bit of a head start. Posh, with family money – something behind them. I came from nothing and I wanted it all.

Oh, decisions, decisions. I was sitting on a potential goldmine. A single photo could launch me, hopefully make me a fortune and let me do anything I wanted with my career. It was a picture that would be syndicated across the world, in all the big magazines, on the net, in all the newspapers: *Hello!*, *OK!*, *Paris Match*, the *National Enquirer*, all of them.

Yes, I would be flushing all my principles down the drain, and turning my back on the likes of Clive and all his integrity. But the way I saw it, I'd be like one of those actresses who does dodgy scenes in crappy TV shows, or loo roll ads, to get noticed by the big film directors. Like Catherine Zeta Jones or Anna Friel; they both started out lowly, took what they could to propel themselves forward. And look at them now. They're doing all right themselves, aren't they? I wouldn't mind having even a bit of what they've got.

The truth was, this photo was my ticket to the future. It was time to open some doors, make some connections and use the luck that had landed in my lap when I first spotted what was happening that day in London, when I'd wandered off for a bit from the annual college Media trip.

I'd been waiting most of my life for the chance to see what was beyond the safe orange glow of home. It was time to seize the chance and get out into the big, bad world.

I contacted the newspapers and made the sale.